Christmas
GRACE

A Regency
Christmas Collection

Christmas
GRACE

JENNIFER MOORE
KRISTA LYNNE JENSEN
ANITA STANSFIELD
CHALON LINTON

Covenant Communications, Inc.

OTHER BOOKS AND AUDIOBOOKS
BY JENNIFER MOORE

REGENCY ROMANCE
Becoming Lady Lockwood
Emma's Campaign
Miss Burton Unmasks a Prince
Simply Anna
Lady Helen Finds Her Song
A Place for Miss Snow
Miss Whitaker Opens Her Heart
Miss Leslie's Secret

THE WAR OF 1812
My Dearest Enemy
The Shipbuilder's Wife
Charlotte's Promise

THE BLUE ORCHID SOCIETY
Solving Sophronia

STAND-ALONE NOVELLAS
"Love and Joy Come to You" in *A Christmas Courting*

Let Nothing You Dismay

BY JENNIFER MOORE

For my own Ben, who I miss like crazy this Christmas.

CHAPTER 1

BEN THOUGHT HE COULD ACTUALLY *feel Camilla Prince's heart breaking as he watched her reaction.*

"Why would he send for you so soon?" She refolded the letter as tears filled her chestnut-brown eyes. "We thought you had years yet."

He handed her a handkerchief as the tears overflowed, leaving shining trails over her pink cheeks. "I know, Millie. I was surprised myself." Ben had assumed once he reached his majority he'd join his father, a financial clerk for the East India Company, in Calcutta. But he was as yet only eighteen. He slipped an arm around her, leaning back against the massive tree trunk, and she buried her face against his shoulder.

"India is so far away," Camilla said in a whisper. "How shall I bear it?"

"Come with me." His heart pounded, both thrilled with the proposition and nervous to see her reaction.

She swatted at his chest and huffed, as only a sixteen-year-old young lady in the midst of a bout of weeping is able. "Don't tease me, Ben."

He held her at arm's length as he watched the shadows of quivering leaves move over her face. "Listen. A few years changes nothing. It only hastens our plan. We'll still be together, Millie. Just sooner."

Camilla wanted to travel the world more than anyone he knew. It seemed nearly every day she had a new destination she'd discovered in one of her father's atlases that she just must visit. Her sketchbook was filled with drawings of jungles, ancient ruins, and exotic animals. This sense of adventure was one of the things Ben loved most about her. A flash of hope lit her face, but it was gone just as quickly as it had appeared. "You know my parents will never allow it."

"They must, if we're married."

"Impossible." She let out her breath in a puff that blew a dark curl from her forehead beneath her bonnet. "Neither of us is of age."

"That does not matter in Scotland." His heart pounded as he said it.

Camilla's eyes went wide. She glanced around as if nervous they'd be overheard. Although they were in the very center of Ellingham beneath the grand elm on the green near the church, the sight of the two of them walking home together on a Sunday afternoon was such a common one that none of the other townsfolk even gave them a second look. "Ben . . ."

"I know it's not the grand wedding you've always dreamed of, with a new gown, flowers, and dancing—"

She put her fingers to his mouth, shushing him. She drew her bottom lip between her teeth, a sign that she was uncertain. But a moment later, a smile spread over her face. "We'll have plenty of time to dance after."

His heart jumped and he smiled back. "We'll dance together every day. Anytime we wish."

He pulled her into an embrace, kissing her quickly before anyone saw, then offered his arm. His heart felt light when she took it.

They continued along the road out of town. "It must be tomorrow then, Millie."

She nodded, her lip drawing back between her teeth. "We'll meet at the bridge?" The bridge crossing the stream that separated their families' properties had been the pair's meeting place for years.

"Midnight." He nodded.

They walked in silence for half an hour, the magnitude of their plans settling heavily, but beneath it was excitement. He and Camilla had talked about marriage of course. He'd never dreamed of marrying anyone else ever since, as an eight-year-old boy, he'd been brave enough to steal a kiss from the pretty girl who lived in Prince Manor. They'd of course assumed a few years remained before they would marry, but his father's letter had forced Ben's hand. Marriage to Camilla . . . he could not imagine his life taking another course. She was his dearest friend, his . . . everything, and he'd loved her since he could remember.

When they reached the bridge, a thrill moved through him. Tomorrow night, they'd meet in this very spot. He'd take the carriage—of course, convincing his guardian, Mr. Norwood, to arrange it would be no problem—and in two days, Camilla Prince would be his bride. He couldn't control the grin that spread over his face. He grabbed her shoulders and kissed her then pulled her against him, resting his chin on her head.

Her arms moved around his middle, feeling familiar and warm. "I love you, Ben."

"You'll not change your mind?"

She shook her head. "Nothing could keep me away."

∼℧∽

Eight years later, Ben stood on the green beside the church, looking up at the old elm tree. He'd thought enough time had passed to erase the ache in his heart, but being back in Ellingham, surrounded by memories of his youth, memories of *her*, brought it all back in a rush.

He shivered and stepped out of the shade, but the winter sun did little to warm him. He'd not remembered England being so cold. But perhaps it was more than the weather that brought a chill.

He remounted his horse and turned along the main road out of town. He had business to attend to. His father's death left an enormous amount of administrative procedures for him to finalize, and of course he'd left this one until last: selling his childhood home. The journey from the center of Ellingham to Lennox House lasted only a quarter of an hour on horseback, but the ride was torture. Every house, each bend in the road, even the very dirt beneath the horse's hooves seemed saturated with memories; and moving through all of them, tainting them like a drop of ink in water, was Camilla's rejection.

He'd waited at the bridge, at first thinking she'd simply been delayed, or perhaps she'd fallen asleep. But as the hours ticked by, the excuses turned into uncertainty, then worry, until finally, the reality of the situation had become clear: she was not coming. Early the next morning, he'd hurried to Prince Manor but was turned away at the door by Nolan, the butler. The family was not accepting visitors.

Ben had never been refused admission before and could only assume Camilla had confessed the entire scheme to her parents. From the harried look on Nolan's typically calm face and the minister's carriage in the drive, it wasn't difficult to conclude the Princes were reprimanding their daughter. Though Ben had never heard them say it aloud, he knew they didn't consider him worthy of Camilla, and any hopes he had of sneaking away with her were dashed.

Camilla Prince had changed her mind, and her rejection hurt worse than Ben could have imagined.

A cold cloud had descended then. He'd returned the carriage, thrown his things into a trunk, and bid farewell to his father's steward, setting off within a few hours for Portsmouth to find a ship to take him to India and his new life.

He'd not looked back, and though it was impossible to keep her completely from his thoughts, he'd done all in his power to do just that until years dulled the ache. But being here, seeing this place—nearly unchanged over the years— brought the pain anew.

Ben shook it off. It was done. Camilla was more than likely far away, married with a child or two. This trip would be good for him. He could sever the last tie that held him to Ellingham and get past this. With any luck, he'd finalize the accounts and say goodbye to this town. Then, as the sole owner of his late father's ruby mine in Karur, he'd take his fortune and settle somewhere. Perhaps a villa in Italy . . .

His thoughts cut off as he approached the bridge and a fresh ache arose, nearly stealing his breath. He urged the horse faster. He would conquer this. And he'd decided the best way was to face it head-on.

He touched the small wooden box in his coat pocket. A silly thing, really, but when he'd seen the item in a dusty Bombay shop—a pencil box, a colorful peacock on the lid inlaid with precious stones—he'd just known Camilla should have it. *It is not inappropriate for an old friend to leave a gift with a woman's parents as he passes through town,* he'd told himself. And in spite of his very gentlemanly intentions, he had to admit to an ulterior motive. Millie's parents had never considered him worthy of her, and he suspected it was this very argument they'd used to convince her not to meet him that night, nor to contact him anytime within the last eight years. His financial situation had improved dramatically; in fact, if one were crass, one would say he was as rich as Croesus now. Wanting to prove himself to Millie's father was beneath him . . . mostly.

He shook his head at the childish thoughts. Tomorrow, all these old feelings and grudges would be set to rest. He'd pay a visit to Prince Manor. Being in the old house again, hearing where Camilla had gone, what she'd done with her life, would be the final step. A closure. He'd be able to move on. As she had.

CHAPTER 2

"STOP WATCHING ME AND TURN your face back where it belongs." Millie was growing more frustrated by the minute.

"I'm sitting on a rock, my nose itches, and I've been holding still for over an hour," Ben complained, a teasing smirk tugging at his lips. "Besides, I like watching you draw. It's far more enjoyable than being the subject."

Millie set down her drawing pad and positioned Ben's head once again. "We've only a bit of time left before the light changes. No more moving, or I'll never get it right." Sitting back on the blanket, she studied the line of his jaw then recreated it on her paper, shading along the edge and adding side whiskers. Ben had only started wearing his long hair pulled back within the last few months, and she had to confess, she liked it a lot. The style accentuated his cheekbones and made him look more . . . well, more like a man. The realization brought a burst of heat to her cheeks.

"And what are you blushing about?" Ben said. "I'm the one being analyzed like a turkey in the butcher's window."

"A turkey who can't keep still," Camilla scolded. She felt flustered. Something that was happening more and more often. She didn't quite understand it. She'd always been perfectly comfortable with Benedict Talbot. But lately things between them had changed, and she struggled to understand why.

She'd noticed little differences. Ben offering his arm when they walked together, instead of just running ahead and trusting her to follow. He'd started complimenting her dresses and offering to carry the basket that held her drawing supplies. Months had passed since he'd put a frog in her hair or teased her about her freckles.

Ben's shoulders seemed broader—perhaps because at fifteen years old, he wore a gentleman's coat—and he stood straight, with a newfound confidence that she found she liked quite a lot, but it was also disconcerting. Was Ben outgrowing their friendship?

"You didn't tell me why you're blushing." She hadn't noticed him move closer until she looked up from her sketch. Ben's head was tipped to the side; his eyes

squinted as he studied her face. He knelt in front of her and gave a half smile, revealing the dimple in one cheek.

Millie's heart tripped.

Ben pinched her chin, causing her to release her lip from between her teeth. An old habit her mother lectured her about constantly. He pulled back into a crouch, rubbing a thumb over the knuckles of his other hand—his own nervous habit.

She looked down and started putting away her charcoals. "I suppose I'll have to finish tomorrow. Perhaps then you'll be more disposed to remaining still."

"Why the urgency?" he asked. His voice was low and serious.

"Well, I'll need to remember how you look, won't I?" She closed the leather flap over her portfolio and put it into her basket. "When you return to school."

He grimaced. Over the summer holiday, the two had had an unspoken pact to avoid speaking of the inevitable end of their time together. He stood and helped her to her feet then folded the blanket she sat on, tucking it into the basket and setting the handle over his arm.

She slipped her hand into the crook of his elbow, and they started back toward her house so she could wash and dress for supper.

"I don't need a drawing to remember you," Ben said after a moment. He spoke without looking at her. "In spite of all your efforts, your curls escape their pins and fall over your forehead. You blow them out of your eyes with a puff of air. You have twenty-seven freckles on your nose and cheeks. Your eyes are the color of rich coffee with just a splash of cream, and in some light, I can see flecks of gold in the irises." He darted his eyes to the side. "When you laugh, your nose wrinkles and your eyes squint, and I can always tell when you're concerned, because you bite your lip."

Camilla felt like she couldn't draw a deep breath. A funny feeling moved through her stomach. She glanced up at Ben and saw his cheeks were a bit red as well.

"I picture you every day," he said, looking straight ahead. His voice had lowered to nearly a whisper. "So I don't forget."

⁓

The memory rushed through Millie's mind as she stared down at the calling card Nolan had just handed her.

Benedict Talbot was here at Prince Manor. Right this very moment. She thought she might be ill. Why had he come? What would he say? What should she say? So many questions swirled through her mind that she started to get dizzy. What if she swooned?

"Of course we'll see Mr. Talbot, Nolan." Millie's mother took the card from her hand. "Please show him in. And send for tea."

"Mother, I—" Millie began.

Her mother's lips pursed and she shook her head. "Now, Camilla, the past is the past. And I hear he's very rich now. He pays us quite an honor by visiting."

"But he mustn't know . . ."

"Of course not, dear."

Footsteps sounded outside the drawing room, and Millie's heart seized. Her mother took her arm and helped her to rise. The pain in her legs and back cleared away her foolish thoughts.

Nolan opened the door. "Mr. Benedict Talbot," he said then stepped aside.

Millie fought back a gasp and hid it by curtsying. If she kept one leg bent and put all her weight on the other, she could lower herself just enough to be proper and rise back up without falling. Her heartbeat was wild.

"Good morning, ladies."

It was him, Ben. Her Ben. Everything about him was so familiar: his voice, the way he inclined his head ending with a little jerk, how he stood with his legs apart and his head tipped the slightest bit, as if waiting for her to speak.

She couldn't speak if she'd wanted to.

"A pleasure to see you, Mr. Talbot," Millie's mother said. "You remember my daughter, Camilla." She held her hand toward a chair. "Please, do sit."

"Thank you." Ben sat.

Millie sank down onto her seat, keeping her face from showing the pain the action caused. The chair's custom cushion made it easier for her to sit comfortably, but maintaining an erect posture still required effort. She tucked back her legs beneath the seat, hoping her skirt concealed their irregularity, and concentrated on breathing calmly.

"What brings you to Ellingham, sir?" Mrs. Prince said, settling back into her chair.

"I am just seeing to estate business, tidying up loose ends, making certain everything is in order as I take possession. My father's holdings were quite diverse, as you may know."

"Am I to understand that the elder Mr. Talbot has passed?"

"Yes, madam."

"I am very sorry to hear it. From the few interactions I had with him, he impressed me as a fine man."

"He was indeed, Mrs. Talbot."

Millie kept her eyes downward. She felt a swell of sorrow for Ben. His father had been his only family.

"And my steward tells me I have sympathies of my own to offer," Ben said. "I am very sorry for your loss. I admired Mr. Prince very much." His words were surprising. Millie's father had tolerated Ben at best, had not kept it a secret that he didn't consider the son of an absent trader a suitable companion for his daughter.

"Thank you," Mrs. Prince said. Millie could hear the sadness in her mother's voice.

"And I extend condolences to you as well, Miss . . . or is it Mrs.?"

Millie's gaze snapped up when she realized Ben was speaking to her. "Miss, sir. And I thank you for your concern."

"So sorry, Miss Prince."

She didn't miss the way Ben's brow rose when he heard that she still retained her maiden name. He'd no doubt expected her to be married. Her stomach sank a bit. He'd not come today expecting to see her, then.

He regarded her with a look she couldn't decipher. As familiar as he'd seemed moments earlier, there were definite changes in Benedict Talbot. For one thing, his skin color was darker, no doubt from living in a hot climate then traveling by ship for the past months. His clothes were different as well. Much finer than she'd seen him wear. Why, the waistcoat must be pure silk, and so beautifully embroidered. She remembered sketching his face, and though much was the same in his overall appearance, the planes of his cheeks had become flattened, and his neck was wider. His side whiskers were thicker and cut off in a deliberate line beneath his ears.

Instead of an attractive youth, he was now an extremely handsome man. But the most noticeable change was in Ben's demeanor. He held himself with a self-assurance she'd not seen before. She felt at the same time proud and apprehensive. If he had any idea her own deficiency . . .

Millie turned her eyes back downward.

Mrs. Julien brought the tea, setting it before Mrs. Prince. Knowing it was difficult for Millie to lean forward to serve the others, her mother poured out.

"And do you mean to remain long in Ellingham?" Mrs. Prince handed a cup to Ben.

He accepted with a nod of thanks and took a sip. "I imagine the business will keep me here a few weeks at least."

"Splendid, then you shall of course attend the Christmas Eve ball."

His eyes widened for an instant then he smiled, the dimple in his cheek showing. "I must admit, in my traveling I've quite lost track of the date. Is Christmas so near?"

Mrs. Prince laughed. "Oh, yes. Christmas Eve is this coming Tuesday."

"The Christmas Eve ball." Ben's eyes looked thoughtful. "I remember."

Mrs. Prince's holiday ball was legendary. The festivities attracted families from miles around, and of course the entire town of Ellingham would attend. Some of Millie's very happiest memories took place at the Christmas Eve ball. She and Ben had danced . . . She swallowed away the memory.

An uncomfortable silence grew, and Millie wondered if he was remembering the two of them dancing as well.

Ben cleared his throat. "You both seem to be in good health."

"Yes, we've been lucky this winter," Mrs. Prince said. "Neither of us has had so much as a sniffle since the weather turned cold."

"Glad to hear it." Ben ran his thumb over his knuckles absently. "And, ah, the manor house looks to be well maintained."

"Oh, yes," Mrs. Prince said. "Thank you."

Ben glanced around the room, and Millie was certain he was planning to take his leave. And something inside her rebelled against it.

"Did you see a tiger?" she blurted out.

Ben blinked. "I beg your pardon, Miss Prince?"

Millie felt a rush of heat spread over her cheeks. "In India. Did you see a tiger?"

The politely curious look on Ben's face softened and a smile grew on his face. "As a matter of fact I did. A few times, though only one posed any sort of threat. Most hid away when they caught sight of people, and I only caught a glimpse here or there."

"You were in danger?"

Ben nodded. "A tiger was attacking a small village north of Calcutta. They call this type of animal a man-eater, you see, once it develops a taste for humans."

Mrs. Prince put her fingers in front of her mouth. "Oh, my."

He darted a look at her, his brow furrowing, perhaps wondering if he should stop speaking, but Millie was desperate to hear the entire tale.

"Continue, Mr. Talbot." She realized, in her eagerness to hear the story, she was barking orders. "If you please," she amended.

"Very well. The animal had already killed two people, and the village sent for help. A Lieutenant Bancroft from the Calcutta regiment invited me to accompany a group of soldiers on a hunt for the animal." He scooted to the front of his chair, leaning forward as he spoke. "Since the tiger was attacking at night, we patrolled the village after dark."

"And did it attack?" Millie leaned forward without thinking then winced at the pain it caused in her hips.

Ben gave a small smirk that turned into a smile, letting her know he planned to draw out the story. "It attacked."

"Oh." Millie clenched her hands together.

"Some of the officers and I were on horseback, while most of the sepoys patrolled on foot. In the darkness, we heard a growl followed by a scream and rushed toward the sounds."

He paused for dramatic effect. "When we arrived a moment later, we found a man torn to ribbons. He'd not even had a chance to shoot his weapon. The tiger turned when we approached, and I must say, I've never seen a more terrifying sight. Its teeth were sharp and long. All of its hair stood on end as it prepared to pounce, and its roar nearly made me drop my gun. The animal was much larger than I'd assumed. About the size of the hearth, I'd wager."

Both Millie and her mother turned to look at the sitting room hearth.

"What did you do?" Millie whispered.

"The lieutenant, a corporal, and I raised our weapons just as it jumped. Did you know a tiger can leap more than six meters?"

Millie shook her head. "You shot it?"

"We shot it. All three of us at the same time as it flew toward Lieutenant Bancroft. I don't know if one bullet alone could have taken down such a massive beast."

Millie and Mrs. Prince both let out a sigh of relief.

Ben shrugged a shoulder. "If you ever care to see it, the animal—or at least his stuffed skin—is in the entry hall of my Calcutta home."

"No . . ." Millie said.

"I swear it." Ben grinned, and in the expression, she recognized the boy she'd known.

"But pursuing such an animal in the dark . . . you must have been terrified."

"One grows used to being out in the dark. The days are so hot that all visits take place in the early morning hours, and most social events are only possible once the sun has gone down."

Mrs. Prince excused herself to speak with the cook, but aside from Ben rising as she left, he and Camilla hardly noticed the interruption.

When he sat, he chose a different chair, next to Millie's. "One of my very favorite things was a nighttime cruise on the Ganges," he said. "*Putallia* boats are shallow and flat-bottomed, and lines of men pull them—like canal barges. Aboard, there is supper, music, and even dancing beneath the stars."

"I imagine it's wonderful."

He nodded. "But I like it best when the boat is silent. The full moon bathes the world in silvery light. The jungle grows right up to the river's edge, and vines hang down, trailing into the water. One can hear jackals, monkeys, the buzzing of insects, the calls of birds. Sometimes even the trumpet of an elephant. Occasionally a temple carved from white stone glows among the trees." He smiled, a faraway look on his face.

"And in the daytime, there is more color, there are more sights, more smells . . . more everything . . . than you can imagine. At first, the sheer mixture was overwhelming. Brightly feathered birds, trees everywhere. Silks, jewels, music, moths the size of dinner plates. It is as if life itself is richer there. I do not imagine a person could visit India and not find himself changed by the experience."

Millie realized she was staring with her mouth agape, drinking in every word that he said. Her longing to travel abroad, to experience the world, filled her so fully that she closed her eyes to hold back the tears. It was a dream not meant to be. She'd long ago made peace with the fact. But hearing Ben describe India rekindled her old yearnings.

"Tell me more," she said, feeling like a child not ready for sleep who asks for another bedtime story. She wished she could lean in her chair, curl up, and just listen.

"One night, a wealthy nabob named Mr. Charles Duncan hosted a party. A caravan of sorts, culminating in a picnic. He procured an entire herd of elephants for our group to ride. You see, everyone is always trying to outdo one another. Perhaps you've seen a drawing of an elephant outfitted with a *howdah*. It's rather like a sofa attached to the animal's back."

Millie nodded. She had seen drawings of the like in one of her father's books.

"The party rode deep into the jungle for nearly an hour. When we arrived, we found our host had arranged an entire ballroom in a jungle clearing. Table-cloths, fine china, fresh flowers, and even a small orchestra playing beneath a starry sky."

She smiled. "It sounds like a fairy story."

"It does indeed."

"The entire experience seems so delightful. I wonder that you ever left the place. You intend to return?"

He nodded. "I imagine I will. I have some ventures there I do not wish to neglect."

"I don't blame you. Ellingham must seem very dull after all your travels."

"Not at all. This town holds a dear place in my heart. I'd forgotten how the pond freezes over. Perhaps I'll ride out tomorrow and throw rocks through the ice." They both smiled at his mention of one of their favorite childhood pastimes.

Ben hesitated, running his thumb over his knuckles. "Would you care to join me?" His eyes flicked to hers.

The change in the mood was nearly palpable, moving from light and comfortable to a reminder of something deeper that they'd both carefully avoided. The air grew thick.

Millie looked down at her clenched hands, feeling angry that she'd let herself fall back into familiarity so easily. "I'm afraid that will not be possible." She looked up, hiding the hurt inside by making her face impassive and feigning a coldness she didn't feel.

He squinted and looked as if he'd ask another question, but instead lifted his chin. And stood.

She had hurt him again. But what was the alternative? Let him know the truth and allow him to be the one to become suddenly aloof? Or even worse, endure his pity?

Her mother entered the room. "Are you leaving, Mr. Talbot?"

"Yes, madam. I'm afraid I must. Thank you for the tea." He turned to Millie. "Farewell, Miss Prince."

"We shall see you tomorrow at church, shall we not?" Mrs. Prince laid a hand on his arm as he passed.

Ben nodded, glancing once again at Millie before he left the room, closing the door behind him.

She tipped over in the chair, leaning to the side to relieve the sitting pressure. Her legs and back were in agony. But that pain was nothing compared to the hurt inside. Her throat grew tight and tears spilled over onto her cheeks.

Her mother hurried to her side, propping pillows behind her. "Oh, my dear, sitting up for such a long time."

"I will be all right, Mother." The words came out in a gasp.

"I'll have Mrs. Julien bring hot bricks for your back and some willow bark tea for the pain."

Millie nodded, unable to speak.

Her mother switched into her role of caregiver, bustling around the room with blankets and tea until she was satisfied that Millie was as comfortable as she could be. She picked up her knitting and sat in the chair beside her, the one Ben had vacated only moments earlier. "Benedict Talbot has certainly changed," Mrs. Prince said tentatively.

Millie didn't answer, fearing her words would come out as sobs.

Taking her silence for assent, her mother continued. "He's grown so handsome and gracious." Her eyes flickered toward Millie's then back to her knitting. "And I hear he's quite rich."

Millie leaned her head on a pillow and prayed Mrs. Julien would hurry with the tea.

"He still seems to like you quite a lot, Camilla. Perhaps it is fate that he should return now. If you play your cards right . . ."

"Mother, men like Mr. Talbot want a whole wife, not a cripple who cannot even sit astride a horse or take a walk through the garden—" Her words choked off. She'd thought she'd finished crying about her injury years ago, but seeing Ben again, remembering all she'd lost, hurt more than any pain her broken body could produce.

CHAPTER 3

THE POLE TUGGED IN BEN'S hand, and he jumped to his feet, turning the reel slowly so the fish wouldn't jerk free. He glanced to the side and saw that Millie had lowered her drawing pad and watched him expectantly. Though she'd seen him catch countless fish over the years, he still felt a rush of nerves as she watched. He wished to impress her.

A flash of scales gleamed near the surface of the pond as the fish struggled, its white spots looking bright against an amber body. A pike then. And a good-sized one at that. The pole bent downward, but he didn't panic and jerk it up lest the fish pull free; he kept reeling steadily and finally pulled the fish from the water. It thrashed at the end of his line, but Ben was ready with the net. With a quick motion, he snatched up the pike and moved up the bank.

"It's a large one," Millie called.

Ben smiled to himself, proud that she'd seen him wrestle such a specimen from the pond. He crouched down and set to work, untangling the fishing line and prying the hook from the fish's mouth.

"Careful," she said, moving closer to stand behind him.

Ben cried out and whipped around, holding up his hand, palm toward him and index finger bent. "It swallowed my finger!"

Millie's eyes widened, but just for an instant until she realized he was teasing. She huffed and crossed her arms. "It would serve you right if it ate off all your fingers."

"And what would you do then, Miss Prince? You would have to bait the hook for me."

She smirked, no doubt ready with a witty retort, but stopped, and her expression grew thoughtful. Something he'd noticed she'd done more often this summer than last. He wondered at the changes he saw in her but supposed there was much about a fourteen-year-old young woman that he didn't understand, as badly as he wanted to.

"I imagine I would."

Ben couldn't keep his surprise from showing. "You'd stick a hook through a wiggling, slimy worm?"

She nodded, though her nose wrinkled at what she'd often indicated to be a repulsive task. "And I'd help with your . . . correspondence and . . . shirt buttons. Things that would be difficult without fingers."

Her voice held a hint of teasing, but there was more, something deeper behind the words; an openness, as if she were confessing something that left her feeling vulnerable.

Ben set the rod and fish-laden net down onto the weeds and took a few steps closer to Millie. His heartbeat sounded loud in his ears. "You'd really do all that for me?"

She tipped her head, and curls dropped down onto her forehead. She blew them away with a puff of air. "Of course I would. I . . ."

Her words trailed off, and Ben considered discovering Camilla Prince's thoughts at that moment to be the most important endeavor he'd ever undertaken.

"You . . . what?" he said.

Millie's cheeks flushed red. "Well, I'm your friend, aren't I? And those are the sorts of things friends do for one another."

He didn't believe for a moment that was what she'd intended to say.

"Is that what you are? My friend?"

"Of course I am, Ben. What else would I be?"

Her voice sounded breathy, and his collar felt tight. He took another step closer. Their interaction had veered from their typical banter and teasing, and suddenly the exchange felt . . . significant. As if their very relationship was changing, and the way the next few moments played out would affect everything between them from now on.

"Millie, might I . . ." He swallowed forcefully and cleared his throat. His voice didn't seem to remember how to function. "Would it be too much to ask . . . Could I kiss you?"

Her eyes flew wide. "You want to kiss me?"

Ben tried to read her expression. She didn't seem put off by the idea, and he took that as a good sign. "Very much."

She drew in a shaky breath and looked down at her fingers. "You know you've kissed me before."

"That was different."

"How?"

"I was eight. I want to kiss you for real this time." Ben felt utterly exposed as he watched her face. Her cheeks had turned a deeper red, if that were even possible. She drew her lip between her teeth and nodded shyly. "I would like that."

Ben stepped closer until only a few inches separated them. He reached for her hand, but she pulled away.

"Your fingers are fishy," Millie whispered.

Ben scrambled down the bank, plunging his hands beneath the water, swishing them around, then wiped them on his trousers as he returned. He clasped her hands in his and bent forward, watching her closely and praying he wouldn't see any refusal in her expression.

Millie turned her face upward, her lashes fluttering as her eyelids closed.

He touched his lips to hers, pressing gently at first, then more firmly. He wished her to know he was in earnest, that the kiss wasn't simply an impulsive thing, but it was important to him. Something he'd wanted to do for eight years since he'd jumped out from behind the library sofa and kissed her the first time.

Her lips were soft and supple. The smell of her skin filled his senses, and—

Ben blinked, jarring himself from the memory as the organ began to play. He hadn't realized the service had ended until the congregation began singing the concluding hymn. He ran a finger under his collar, sweating despite the draft, and glanced to where Millie sat at the front of the church. He couldn't see her, of course, with the people between them standing to sing.

Though he'd arrived early, she'd already been seated in the front of the church with her mother. He didn't know why he had hoped to catch her before she went inside. Of course, he wasn't planning to sit with her and Mrs. Prince in their family pew. Knowing that he'd hurried to church just to catch a glimpse of her aggravated him. *I am moving on*, he reminded himself.

The service ended and the congregation made their way through the aisles toward the doors. Millie and her mother remained in their seats. Perhaps she was avoiding him.

Ben rose and walked toward the church doors. Stepping outside, he put his hat on his head and shivered. England was downright cold in the winter. He moved to stand in a patch of sunlight in the churchyard and rubbed the wooden figurine in his pocket out of habit.

He'd been foolish to think the two of them could just slip back into their former relationship—it was impossible after what had happened. His offer to take her riding attested to it. Why had he made himself vulnerable again? So she could reject him a second time?

The confusion of his head telling him one course and his heart insisting on another frustrated him. He'd had a definite purpose when he'd gone to

Prince Manor the day before, but seeing Millie again had made him question his resolve.

She had, of course, changed in eight years. Parts of her figure had filled out and others had slimmed, transformed by womanhood. He'd been shocked by how beautiful she'd become. But of course he'd not imagined any less.

Her manner had been restrained when compared to the impetuous young woman he'd known, but he'd seen the same intelligence in her eyes, the same liveliness he'd so adored. In spite of himself, Ben smiled as he remembered her hands clenching and her eyes widening as she'd listened to his story about the tiger. Naturally he'd known such a tale to be inappropriate for two women, but he'd recognized Millie's longing to hear more, remembered her fascination with tales of exotic adventure, especially when danger was involved. He rolled his eyes at the unabashed attempt to amaze her with his boastful story full of bravado.

He tipped his hat and nodded to a passing family.

The visit the day before had felt like stepping onto a frozen pond, moving ever so carefully, unsure of just what might break through the ice. Beneath the cordiality, the conversation, even the laughter, were unspoken questions. He could feel them hovering just beneath the surface.

He could see through the cool façade Millie had tried to project. She was the same girl with a mind full of questions, who longed to see the world and have adventures of her own. So, why hadn't she? And why did he feel such a need to find out?

Though he tried to avoid it, the truth was obvious. His feelings for Millie were very much the same as they'd ever been. Distance, time, even her rejection—eight years ago, and again yesterday—had not managed to extinguish his affection.

It was obvious that she did not share his feelings, and knowing it hurt. If he was going to move past this, leave his feelings behind and carry on with his life, he needed to speak with her. She owed him an explanation for . . . everything. For not meeting him at the appointed time, not sending word then or ever in the long years following. Perhaps apprehension had prevented her. It was a perfectly reasonable reaction for a sixteen-year-old girl to an elopement. But why had she kept it from him? If her parents had found out and forbidden it, he should have been informed. If he had done something to offend her, she should have told him. He could demand that much from her, he reasoned. Perhaps hearing her utter the words would make his heart realize that his mind was right. He could move forward and leave Ellingham and Camilla Prince behind.

But in order to do that, he needed to speak to her alone. Perhaps she would allow him to walk home with her. He leaned to the side, peeking back into the church. Millie and her mother still sat on their pew.

"Are you looking for my father, Mr. Talbot?" The voice came from behind.

He turned to find the speaker and saw a young woman standing before him. She was very pretty, with blonde curls, pink cheeks and lips, and wide blue eyes. A classic English beauty.

She knew his name, but Ben didn't recognize her at all. How very unconventional for a young lady to approach a single gentleman alone. And he wasn't sure how to reply. They'd not been introduced, after all. But he couldn't just ignore her or pretend he hadn't heard. Who was she? And why did she assume he knew her father? He studied her closer, trying to dredge up any hint of memory that might include this person.

"Pardon me, miss. I don't believe we've been introduced."

Her round cheeks turned even pinker. "We have, but not for quite some time. I'm Beatrice Delaney."

"Ah, the minister's daughter. I apologize. I did not recognize you."

She fluttered her lashes and gave a sweet smile. "I was very young when we last met. I don't blame you for not recognizing me."

Ben figured a bit of arithmetic in his head. Based on her age now, Beatrice Delaney must have been quite young indeed. "A pleasure to make your acquaintance . . . again, Miss Delaney."

She bounced in a small curtsy. Her eyelashes fluttered some more, and Ben fought back a groan. This young woman—girl—could not have been older than sixteen.

"Father will be meeting with parishioners. But he'll be home for luncheon if you'd care to call this afternoon."

A moment passed before Ben understood what she was saying. She thought he was waiting in the churchyard to speak to the minister. A logical conclusion, he decided. "Perhaps I shall, Miss Delaney." He noticed the churchyard was nearly empty and did not like the implications that might be drawn if he were to remain here alone with this young lady.

She pointed down the lane on the other side of the church. "You remember where the parsonage is, don't you, Mr. Talbot?"

"Yes." Ben offered his arm. "Shall I see you home, miss?"

Her smile grew, lifting up her round cheeks and making her face beam. "Thank you, sir." She slipped her hand beneath his elbow, and they started up the lane.

Twenty minutes later, snow started to fall as Ben strode alone up the road to Lennox house. *A nice girl*, he thought. With emphasis on the word *girl*. She had chattered nonstop, and he had to admit his mind wandered after only a few minutes. He remembered her speaking about inviting him to the parsonage for supper one of these evenings, and of course about the Christmas Eve ball. He thought he might have committed to a few dances, but he wasn't entirely certain.

The sounds of hooves and a carriage approaching behind made him glance back and step to the side of the road to allow the conveyance to pass. But instead of continuing past, the carriage stopped.

Mrs. Prince leaned out, holding open the door. "The day is cold, Mr. Talbot. Please allow us to transport you home."

Ben glanced at Millie, but she just gave a polite nod.

"Thank you," he said as he climbed into the carriage. It wasn't quite the private meeting he'd hoped for, but he would take it. And he was grateful for the warmth of the equipage.

Mrs. Prince moved to sit on the bench next to Millie, and Ben stepped inside, sliding onto the bench facing them. He pulled the door closed and tapped his walking stick on the roof, and the carriage was off.

"I appreciate it, ladies." Ben brushed snow from the top of his hat. "And how did you enjoy the sermon today?"

"Very nice," Mrs. Prince said. "Wasn't it, Camilla?"

Millie gave another polite nod. The usual brightness was gone from her eyes. She appeared tired, even a bit upset. Ben hadn't heard much of the sermon, and he wondered if the minister had said something that bothered her.

He set the hat on his knee and laid his walking stick over his legs, knowing they had only a little time before arriving at his house. If he was going to learn anything about Camilla, it would need to be now. "I must apologize for monopolizing the entire conversation at our last visit. I was rather carried away talking about India. If you please, Miss Prince, what has occupied your time these past years?" And how was it that a beauty like her, with her wit and love of life, hadn't married?

"I've been occupied with my drawings." She gave a shrug as if uncertain how he'd react to the admission.

"Now, don't downplay your accomplishments, my dear," Mrs. Prince said. She leaned forward, toward Ben. "Camilla has studied beneath the tutelage of Marcel Reynaud."

Ben lifted his brows, certain, by her expression, that he was supposed to be impressed with the name, but he didn't have the faintest idea who Marcel Reynaud was.

"He's a French artist," Millie said, still looking tentative.

"He's a *master* artist from the *Grande Académie d'art* in Paris," her mother said, her tone both scolding and filled with pride. "Monsieur Reynaud saw a drawing of Camilla's on a visit to London. An old family friend, Lady Spencer, was quite taken with the picture when she was last in Ellingham, and Camilla gave it to her when she departed. She displays it very prominently in her sitting room. A picture of a rose covered in dew, is it not, Camilla?"

Millie nodded. She raised her gaze shyly as if anticipating Ben's reaction.

"You see, Monsieur Reynaud was so impressed with Camilla's talent that he journeyed immediately to Ellingham to meet her for himself." Mrs. Prince gave a satisfied nod.

"That's wonderful," Ben said. And he meant it. "You must have become very proficient."

"Thank you," Millie said. "Of course, there is always more to learn."

"Monsieur Reynaud remained for months and actually offered Camilla a position as his assistant at the académie. He hoped she would eventually replace him."

Ah, perhaps this was the answer to one of Ben's questions at least. It would certainly explain why she'd not married if she was busy teaching. "And how did you like Paris?"

"I have not gone." Camilla's gloved hands were clenched tightly in her lap. "Monsieur Reynaud comes to tutor me in the summer when the school is on holiday."

Instead of the understanding he'd expected, her answer caused questions to grow exponentially in Ben's mind. Why had she not gone to Paris? Was something keeping her here? Did she intend to take the position? And the one that made his gut heavy: Were she and Marcel Reynaud in love? The only question he could think to ask was, "Why not?"

Camilla looked toward the carriage window, but not before Ben saw a flash of sorrow in her eyes. It was so intense that an anguish grew inside him in response. Millie was grieving. For her father? Or did she miss her French tutor? What could possibly cause her such pain?

She lifted her chin as if bracing herself. "I have kept quite occupied here in Ellingham," she said. "I teach a drawing class on Friday afternoons for a few children in town."

Teaching youngsters to scribble on paper hardly sounded like a sufficient justification for turning down an opportunity of such magnitude. There was obviously more to the story. More Ben didn't understand. And he feared it had to do with this Marcel Reynaud. Had he broken her heart? Ben couldn't imagine any other occurrence that could have brought such pain to Millie's eyes, or any other reason that at twenty-four she wasn't married.

Aside from the creak of the wheels and the sound of hooves, the carriage had grown quiet. A heavy quiet, filled with questions both unasked and unanswered. He glanced at Mrs. Prince and saw that her eyes were shining. She watched her daughter with an expression of pity that was nearly as painful to see as Millie's own grief-filled eyes.

The carriage arrived at Lennox house, and Ben climbed out, bidding the women farewell and promising to attend the ball in two days. His mind turning, he made his way through the halls to the library and poured a drink. He sank down onto a leather chair in front of the hearth and stared into the fire.

What was Camilla's secret? And would discovering it mean heartache for both of them?

CHAPTER 4

MILLIE CREPT TO HER BEDCHAMBER door and pressed her ear against it. The house was quiet. She lit the candles in her room and dressed in her very favorite gown. Dark-blue velvet with cream-colored ribbons. She knew her parents intended this dress to be among the gowns she took to London in a few months for her coming out Season. She stepped into new silk dancing slippers, admiring the embroidery as she fastened them, then stepped back to study herself in the mirror.

Did she look like a bride? A nervous giggle rose in her throat. By tomorrow, she'd be Mrs. Benedict Talbot. Her breathing came faster and her knees felt shaky. She sat on her dressing table stool. "It's just a case of nerves," she whispered to her reflection.

She loved Ben, adored him with every bit of her soul. Bidding him farewell as he left for school in the fall had hurt her heart so badly that she knew she could not endure his leaving for India without her. He would be gone for years . . . perhaps forever.

Her shaking calmed, but her jumping heart did not. It was perfectly reasonable for a young woman to be nervous as she prepares for her wedding. She wished she could tell her parents, particularly her mother, but they would of course forbid it. Her father especially did not consider Benedict Talbot to be an adequate choice for his only child, heiress to Prince Manor and the surrounding acreage. How could her father not understand?

That settles it, she thought, standing. I will be married to Ben, and we will sail to India. She sighed, glancing toward the picture book beside her bed. How often had she scrutinized each drawing, fantasizing about what it would be like to travel the world? Soon she wouldn't have to dream about the world outside of Ellingham. Ben would take her on adventures. She would see a real jungle, smell the exotic spices in a market, and feed fruit to a monkey. She'd do all of it with the person she loved very most in the world. Her Ben.

Her nervousness abated, replaced with anticipation, and she fetched the prepared valise and cloak from her closet. Half an hour remained before midnight, and she needed to hurry.

Millie left the letter she'd written on the dressing table where her lady's maid would find it and pushed open her window. Cool air rushed in, and she was glad for it. The bout of nerves had made her a bit warm. She dropped her cloak and valise out the window, pulling back inside and listening to see if the noise roused anyone. When nothing happened, she climbed up onto the windowsill. She glanced back one last time, bidding farewell to her childhood bedchamber, and then leaned out to grasp onto the closest limb.

The old oak tree felt familiar. She could practically climb up and down through the thick branches in her sleep. She held onto the limb and swung her legs out to catch onto a thicker branch. But it went wrong. Her new slippers gave no traction; instead, her feet slid along the branch but couldn't plant firmly.

Millie swung for an instant, her legs scrambling to find purchase, then her hands lost their grip.

She hit the ground and her body made a crunching sound. Pain shot from each leg, and her back cracked.

❧

Millie woke with a scream that brought her mother and Mrs. Julien running. She reassured them that all was well as they fussed and rearranged her pillows. Then, as soon as they left her alone, she allowed the tears to flow. Over the past eight years, she'd had the nightmare numerous times, but it never faded in intensity. The pain, the terror, all of it, was as distinct as the day it happened.

She lay awake, memories flooding over her. The months following the accident were blurry in her mind, disjointed images surfacing from a haze of laudanum. Her mother's weeping, her father's worry, the doctor's painful procedures as he tried to realign crushed bone. She had been recommended to a surgeon in London who had explained that in addition to her legs being broken, her spine had suffered irreparable damage. She'd likely never walk again.

Millie had refused to believe the diagnosis. Especially when it meant a footman was required to carry her up and down the stairs. Months of painful exercises turned into years, retraining her muscles to work around their new frame and making excruciatingly slow progress. But she'd not given up. The humiliation of the footman coming every morning and evening to convey her to and from her bedchamber was all the motivation she'd needed.

She could walk now, but not without assistance. Though lately she'd been able to move for short distances with the help of a walking stick. It didn't seem like much, but it was a small victory. And to Millie, the independence was worth the pain as she hobbled on uneven legs.

That slip off an oak tree's limb had cost her the one thing she'd wanted most—being with Ben. Knowing that he'd left for India without her was painful, but knowing he still remained—at her insistence—unaware of the reason she'd not met him that night hurt worse. He had no doubt thought himself abandoned; assumed Millie had changed her mind. She knew he'd be unable to forgive her and that he'd assuredly think ill of her the remainder of his life. But it was better than the alternative. She would not bear his pity or his guilt. Ben was too honorable to have walked away from a crippled fiancée. He would have remained with her, trapped and deprived of a full, rich life.

Ben deserved a whole woman instead of an invalid.

And now he'd returned just in time for the Christmas Eve ball, and Millie thought it the worst torture ever devised.

She and Ben had adored the ball. It was one of the few times a young man and woman of their ages could dance together. And they both loved to dance. She'd always taken special care getting ready, hoping he'd compliment her appearance. And he never disappointed.

She imagined him tonight, dressed in black, whirling among the other dancers. Would he waltz? She pictured silly Beatrice Delaney in Ben's arms while she herself watched from a cushioned chair on the side of the ballroom, and her heart ached.

Enough was enough. Millie wiped away her tears and slowly pulled herself to a sitting position. The hour was still early; the upstairs maid hadn't even lit the fire in her hearth. But she knew she'd not be returning to sleep. She rubbed the base of her spine, thinking she should ask Mrs. Julien for a heated brick this afternoon before the festivities. She'd found that heat, applied just right, eased some of the nerve pain.

In the years before the accident, she'd have spent the day supervising the gathering of greenery to decorate the windowsills and door frames. Wreaths, ribbons, mistletoe, even kissing boughs—she'd loved arranging all of it. She was particularly fond of decorating the table with trails of ivy and tucking clumps of holly with bright-red berries among the candles. But now she would simply direct the servants from a wheeled chair.

Though she knew her mother still looked forward to the ball, Millie dreaded it. It was just one more opportunity for people to pat her hand, ask after her

health, and shake their heads as they gave her pitying looks. Most of the town
didn't quite know the nature of her injuries. And she was happy to keep it that
way, though it did take a bit of planning—such as arriving early to church—and
maintaining the secret turned her into a bit of a recluse.

At least she had her art to occupy her time and mind. If it weren't for
Monsieur Reynaud and his lessons, she didn't know what she'd do.

She reached for her dressing gown, sliding her arms into the sleeves. There
was plenty of work to do, and feeling sorry for herself would change nothing.

That afternoon, Millie studied herself in the mirror. The gown she'd chosen
was a deep-red satin with white lace at the collar that matched perfectly the
long gloves that covered her arms and elbows. Festive, but nothing that would
draw too much attention. Her lady's maid assisted her as she descended the
stairs. Each step caused a burst of pain, but she refused to be carried. Once she
reached the entry hall, she was exhausted, and Nolan instructed a footman to
bring a chair for her to rest on until she'd be expected to greet the guests.

As per tradition, the Christmas Eve ball began early in the evening, giving
families time to return home and light their own yule log and prepare for
the following day. Though the ball had begun with only a few close families,
within a few years, the entire town was invited, and in the years following, the
invitations spread to include families from neighboring villages. As an open
ball, Mrs. Prince's party did not require a formal invitation.

Years ago, neighbors had brought trays of sweets to share, and that tradition
had grown as well, the cooks of various households attempting to best one
another in friendly competition. Millie had already seen the fairy cakes and
pastries Mrs. Julien had made, sitting in a place of honor at the center of the
long draped table. She'd truly outdone herself.

"Oh, Camilla, don't you look elegant?" Mrs. Prince walked gracefully down
the stairs. Her own dress of embroidered gold silk sparkled in the candlelight,
and she wore a fox stole around her shoulders.

"Thank you, Mother. You look very beautiful too."

Sounds of the orchestra tuning their instruments came from the ballroom,
and maids rushed about on last-minute orders from the butler or cook.

Mrs. Prince swept a critical gaze around the entry hall and finally gave a
satisfied nod. She came toward Millie and offered an arm to help her stand.
"And won't it be nice to see a particular gentleman neighbor of ours tonight?"

The sound of horses and voices outside the doors saved Millie from having
to answer. She moved with her mother across the hall and took her place beside
the doorway to the ballroom. A footman returned the chair and brought Millie's
walking stick, discreetly placing it against the doorframe behind her.

Mrs. Prince gave a nod to Nolan. The butler glanced toward a waiting line of maids ready to take cloaks and hats then opened the door. As if he'd pulled a stopper from a bottle, people poured in, and laughter and chatter echoed through the hall. The music began, and the Christmas Eve ball was officially underway.

Millie released her mother's arm and stood on her own, balancing carefully. She nodded and curtsied and smiled, subtly shifting her weight when the ache in one leg became too much. She reprimanded herself when her gaze strayed to the door, and brought her attention back to the smiling woman before her, nodding and agreeing that it was indeed the most anticipated event in Ellingham.

She shifted again, wishing she could just sit for a moment and press her knuckles into her back. Nearly an hour of welcoming guests began to blur into one endless greeting of Happy Christmas and wishes for a delightful holiday as she wondered just how much longer before her legs became too tired to support her.

"Happy Christmas, Mrs. Prince."

This voice stood out from the noises around her, and Millie employed every ounce of her self-control to shake the hand she held and curtsy instead of snapping her eyes toward where Ben stood speaking to her mother. She watched him from the corner of her eye as he kissed her mother's hand and complimented the decorations.

A moment later, he took her hand, pressing a kiss on the back of her fingers. He leaned close. "Happy Christmas, Millie."

She blinked at his familiar use of her nickname and glanced around, but with the other noise in the hall, it appeared nobody else had heard. "I am very glad you could come, Mr. Talbot."

His brows ticked upward at the formality of her address, but his smile did not waver. He held her gaze. "You look beautiful."

Though her mother had said nearly the same thing mere hours earlier, hearing the words in Ben's deep voice sent heat skittering over her skin. She pulled away her hand, though she was very tempted to return the compliment. Ben looked exceedingly handsome in a black coat and white cravat. He wore a black silk waistcoat with black thread embroidery. "Thank you," she said.

"And if I might—" he started to say, but his words were cut off by a bouncing blonde mass of ringlets that somehow managed to insert itself between them.

"Mr. Talbot!" Beatrice Delaney grabbed onto his arm. It seemed the minister was a bit negligent when it came to instructing his daughter in matters of propriety. "I am so glad you've come."

"It is very nice to see you again, Miss Delaney." Ben gave a sharp nod.

Mr. Delaney finished speaking to Mrs. Prince and turned to Millie as Beatrice pulled Ben out of the way. "Happy Christmas," Millie said, sounding monotonous to her own ears. She glanced toward Ben but saw he was walking into the ballroom with Beatrice on his arm.

A sadness settled onto her shoulders, making her feel heavy, just as she'd felt when she'd seen them walking together toward the parsonage on Sunday. She leaned toward her mother. "Perhaps we should join the guests in the ballroom now."

Mrs. Prince's brows pulled together in a concerned look. "You've grown very pale, my dear." She looked back to the guests still arriving, but the crowd had thinned. "Nolan is here," she said, nodding toward the butler.

He immediately joined them, standing close enough to help Millie if she should need.

Mrs. Prince squeezed Millie's hand then entered the ballroom and gave a signal to the orchestra director. Immediately the music changed, indicating the dancing was about to begin.

The rest of the guests hurried into the ballroom, and Millie and Nolan were alone, for the moment anyway.

Millie nearly collapsed into his arms as he helped her cross the floor to a discreet door that led to the servant's hallway. Once the door closed behind them, she sank into the wheeled chair, her legs shaking from the exertion.

Nolan pushed the chair through the kitchens and down the servants' hall until he arrived at a door that led into the ballroom. He moved around to stand in front of her. "Are you certain you're well enough, miss?" He gave the same concerned, brows-furrowed expression she'd just seen from her mother.

She nodded, grimacing as a spasm of pain twisted in her back. She let out a heavy breath, exhausted by the effort. "Yes, just let me rest a moment."

CHAPTER 5

BEN STRODE UP THE PATH to Prince Manor. Knowing carriages would clog the drive, they had opted to walk to the Christmas Eve ball. He glanced to the side and smiled, pleased to be attending this year with his father instead of with his dull guardian, Mr. Norwood. Five years had passed since Mr. Talbot had left England and his eight-year-old son behind to begin a career in India, and Ben had missed him terribly. Mr. Norwood was warmhearted, but the old man was no substitute for a family.

The two climbed the steps and stepped through the doors into an entry hall. A maid took their cloaks and hats, and Ben scanned the crowded area, looking for . . . ah, there she was. His heart warmed, and he smiled as he walked with his father toward the Princes.

He greeted Mr. and Mrs. Prince then took Millie's hand, bowing formally. She giggled and curtsied. Curls fell over her forehead and she blew them away with a frustrated puff of air.

"Ben! I have hardly seen you this entire holiday." She pouted her lip.

"I know, but my father . . ."

"Of course you wish to spend time with him. I understand." She folded her arms. "But two entire weeks in London?"

He nodded, unsure of what to say. He didn't like thinking he'd disappointed her.

She couldn't hold the pout for long, and her face lit up in curiosity. "And what was it like?"

"Crowded. And noisy."

"But you enjoyed it?"

He nodded again. He had enjoyed spending the time with his father, attending plays and visiting offices of businessmen. He'd felt important when his father had introduced him, and he liked wearing his new jackets and looking the part of an adult.

"Did you see the king?"

Ben laughed. "No."

"Well, the holiday was not the same without you." The pout returned. She glanced up when Mr. Talbot approached, and curtsied prettily. "Happy Christmas, Mr. Talbot. I hope you enjoyed London."

"I did, actually. Although I believe my son quite missed his friend." He smiled. "Thank you for sharing him with me. His company was very enjoyable." Mr. Talbot placed a hand on Ben's shoulder and winked at his son. Ben stood taller, proud at his father's compliment.

"Shall we, son?" Mr. Talbot tipped his head toward the ballroom.

Ben nodded and smiled at Millie. He'd find her once she and her parents finished welcoming the remainder of the guests.

As he turned, she grabbed onto his arm. She took his hand, and he felt something pressed against his palm. "Happy Christmas," she said, a mischievous twinkle in her eye.

"Happy Christmas, Millie."

An hour later, Ben hurried into the library. Millie's note had told him to meet her during the waltz. Which was quite a clever idea, when he thought about it. The dance was still quite a novelty, especially in the country, and even a bit scandalous. He'd heard whispers of both anticipation and disapproval that Mrs. Prince would have such a dance at her ball. Of course, once the music began, all eyes were on the dance floor. None of the party guests would notice the absence of two young people.

Millie waited inside on the sofa, all ribbons and curls in her Christmas gown. She smiled when he entered and held up a small box covered in gold paper and tied with a ribbon. "I have a Christmas gift for you."

Ben was taken aback. He'd not received a Christmas gift since he was a small child. He sat beside her. "But I do not have a gift for you."

She pushed the box into his hands. "Don't be a goose. Just open it." She bit her lip, and her eyes were bright with anticipation. She bounced a bit on the sofa, clasping her hands together.

Ben untied the ribbon and removed the paper. He opened the lid of the box and drew out a small wooden figurine. A fox. From nose to tail, the figure was no longer than his small finger. It was painted in detail. "Did you make this, Millie?"

She grinned, bouncing again. "I carved it from a branch of the oak tree outside my window. I know the proportions are a bit off; the head is too large, and one leg is fatter than the others . . ."

He held up a hand to stop her words. "It is perfect." He turned it over, noting the details, and his heart felt full. "I cannot believe you made this."

"I know you will go on the fox hunt with the men this year, since your father has come."

The thoughtfulness behind the gift touched him and for a moment, he was utterly speechless. His eyes itched and he cleared his throat. Weeping was utterly out of the question. He closed his fingers around the fox and pressed it to his heart in a way that he hoped looked gallant. He took her hand. "I will treasure it always."

An idea occurred to him. He rose and pulled her up with him. "I do have a gift for you."

"There is no need, Ben. My parents have plenty . . ." He shook his head and pulled her closer to the door where they could hear the music from the ballroom on the floor below.

He slipped the fox into his pocket and gave a formal bow. "Camilla Prince, may I have this dance?"

Her brows lifted and her mouth formed an O. But after an instant, a smile took its place. She dipped in a deep curtsy and took his hand, placing her other hand on his shoulder.

Ben laid a hand on her waist and counted the beats in his head. Down-up-up, 1-2-3, *and stepped back. Millie imitated his movement, and as they began, she watched her feet, lip clenched in her teeth. Of course she'd not been taught how to waltz, and Ben had only learned from some of the older boys at Eton. She followed his lead, and he twirled her, albeit clumsily, around the library. Amidst their laughter, toes were stepped on, and once they crashed into a low table, but Ben's heart soared with the music, and after it ended, he pulled his closest friend into an embrace. She embraced him in return, her curls tickling his nose. "Happy Christmas, Millie," he said. And it was. The happiest he'd known.*

⤖

The first notes of the waltz brought back the memory so forcefully that Ben could do nothing but stand stupidly for a moment as emotions welled up inside. He searched the room again, and this time, at last, he saw her.

Millie sat on a chair in a far corner of the ballroom. How had he not seen her enter? Her hair curled softly around her face and shoulders, and she positively glowed in the beautiful dress. He walked around the edges of the room and finally reached her.

She looked up when he approached and inclined her head. "Mr. Talbot." Her hands were clenched on the arms of the chair, and she held herself stiffly. Not an encouraging sight.

Ben bowed. "Would you grant me the honor of a dance, Millie?"

Her lips compressed and she breathed heavily through her nose. Swallowing hard, she looked away. "No, Mr. Talbot."

Her reaction and answer felt like a punch to the gut. Ben clenched his jaw, suddenly feeling furious, not only at her latest snub but for the last eight years of heartache. He pulled an empty chair toward her and sat, leaning close.

"And am I to receive no explanation for your refusal? For *both* of your refusals?" He knew his voice was sharp but wasn't able to keep it calm. Eight years of wondering, doubting himself, feeling betrayed, hurt, angry—it all came to a head, and he clenched his fists to keep from shouting.

Millie kept her eyes averted and just shook her head. Her face was extremely pale, and she seemed livid. Which was preposterous. *He* was the one who'd been rejected, deserted by his fiancée without one word of explanation. And here, she'd refused to dance.

"Your dislike of me must be quite intense, miss, if the suggestion of a dance is so repulsive that you'd forego any further offers for the remainder of the night."

She swallowed again, her shoulders shaking, but she did not look at him.

"You could have sent word, a note . . . anything . . . What happened to you? Did I . . ." He shook his head. "At times, I see the girl I recognize in your eyes, but it's as if you're hiding her away, not wanting to reveal the truth that she's still there. But you are her. I know it." He could hear a whimper in his voice and stifled it. "So will you tell me why, Millie?"

"You're wrong," she said. Her voice was calm, controlled. She turned toward him, holding herself very stiffly. "I am not the same girl. And I cannot give you an explanation."

Ben pulled back, his anger causing his chest to burn. He stood and clamped his jaw shut, holding back the biting remarks on the tip of his tongue.

"Mr. Talbot, there you are. And good evening, Miss Prince." Beatrice Delaney joined them.

Ben did not spare another glance for Millie. His emotions were so raw that he feared if he did he would either break a piece of furniture or collapse into tears. Instead, without a word, he took Miss Delaney in his arms and whirled her onto the dance floor.

⸺⸱⸺

Two hours later, Ben gathered his cloak and hat in the entry hall and stepped out into the cold winter night. He'd quickly realized that waltzing as a form of anger management was ineffective and petty. And he felt guilty giving Miss Delaney the impression that his feelings for her were anything more than mere friendliness. So, once the waltz ended, he spent the remainder of the evening playing at cards with some of the other gentlemen and wishing Mrs. Prince's Christmas punch was strong enough to numb his feelings. He hadn't wanted to cause any speculation or insult to his hostess by departing before it was polite to do so.

He was foolish for coming in the first place. Not just to the Christmas Eve ball, but to Ellingham in general. There was nothing but heartache for him in this town. First his mother had died, then his father had left for India, then Millie . . .

Well, at least he did not need to speculate any longer. He had the closure he needed; though incomplete, it was enough. Millie did not retain feelings for him. She hadn't pined for him, missing him every day as he had her. She could not even bear to stand up with him at a public dance. She disliked him so much that she could not bring herself to extend that basic courtesy.

Ben didn't want to see her at the Christmas church service or chance another meeting in the small town. There was nothing left to his business that his steward could not do by correspondence. He would leave Ellingham for good, and he would do it tonight.

He stomped through the snowy field. Why had he chosen to walk? The night air bit at his skin. He pulled his cloak tighter around him and felt something heavy in the pocket. The pencil box. *Blast.*

He stopped, debating what to do. He could toss it into the pond, of course, or send it with his steward in a few days, but he'd wrapped it and even found a bit of ribbon in town, making it a Christmas gift.

He wavered, questioning his true intent. Was he planning to give a gift out of spite? He'd certainly danced with Miss Delaney for that reason. But the pencil box . . . He'd purchased it years earlier, knowing it should belong to Millie. A part of his heart was intact enough to wish for her to have it. He knew she would love it.

He turned back toward the manor. Perhaps his intentions were a bit unpleasant—he'd have liked to believe he was above such an intent, but he wasn't completely certain. He strode back through the front doors, open as another family exited, and crossed the entryway to the ballroom.

The sight before him made Ben freeze in his tracks. Nolan, the old butler, and a footman were helping Millie into a wheeled chair. Her few steps were uneven, and her face contorted in pain as she moved.

"Millie?"

The three stopped, looking at him with shocked expressions.

"Go away, Ben."

Her voice was hardly more than a sob. Her use of his name jarred him into action, and he hurried across the room toward her, shaking off the footman's hand as he tried to stop him.

Millie's face was wet with tears. She slumped to the side, both hands on one arm of her chair, as if sitting straight for one moment longer was more than she could bear. She seemed small, defeated. She let out a breath, seeming exhausted. "I didn't want you to see me like this."

He sank to his knee in front of her, setting the package onto the floor and putting a hand over hers. "Why?"

The servants stepped back toward the doorway, giving the pair privacy.

A tear dripped off her cheek. "Isn't it obvious? I knew you'd react just like this. With pity."

Ben pulled a handkerchief from his pocket and wiped at her cheeks. "Compassion isn't the same as pity, Millie." He studied her, trying to understand. Why hadn't he seen it before? The stiff way she sat, the pain in her eyes, remaining in her pew long after church services were finished, and refusing to dance. Something had happened to her, had harmed her. And it all began to make sense. "This is why you didn't come."

She closed her eyes. "I tried, Ben, but I fell . . . the tree . . ."

His heart ached, and he rubbed his eyes. "If I'd known—"

"If you'd known, you'd have given up everything. Your dreams of India, of traveling the world, of being with your father. You'd have stayed and cared for me and married me out of a sense of honor, but you wouldn't have been happy."

"Why wouldn't I be happy?" He genuinely didn't understand. Of course he'd have cared for her.

"Ben, I can hardly walk. My body is broken. I can't do all the things we used to do or the things we dreamed of. I'm damaged beyond repair."

"And why should any of that matter? You're my Millie."

She gave him a disbelieving look and took the handkerchief from his hand, rubbing it beneath her eyes.

He shifted, drawing closer and leaning to catch her gaze. "Let me tell you about my travels. Everything, the pyramids in Egypt, the ruined temples of Greece, Indian jungles, snake charmers . . . each experience felt meaningless because you were not with me. I constantly wondered: How would Millie like this? What details would her artist eyes notice? What would she say? Would she try this strange food? Would she shy away from this animal?"

He lifted her hand, brushing a kiss over her knuckles. "You were with me whether you knew it or not. Nothing was the same without you. Nothing mattered. I felt like I was missing part of myself and thought that time would change it, that it would become easier, but it didn't. You belong with me."

"I'm not a suitable wife, Ben. I don't even know if I'll be able to bear children. And what kind of mother would I be anyway?"

Ben held up his hand, palm toward him and index finger bent.

She drew together her brows and gave him a questioning look.

"Remember the pike? I told you it ate my finger, and do you remember what you said?"

She shook her head, but her eyes didn't meet his. She remembered.

"You said you'd bait the hook for me. You'd fasten my buttons and do my correspondence."

"But—"

"Didn't you mean it?"

"Of course I meant it. But it's not the same, Ben."

"It's exactly the same. But with no worm involved." He gave a grimace, trying to elicit a smile and was rewarded by a very small one. "What if it was me who'd been injured, Millie? Would you leave me?"

Her lip trembled, and more tears fell from her eyes. "No."

It was exactly the word he'd hoped to hear. She was softening. His heart began racing, and tears of his own filled his eyes. He grasped her other hand. "We can go to Paris. I'll help you. If you want to work at the art school with Monsieur Reynaud, we'll live there. If you want to travel to India, I'll take you. I'll carry you across the entire desert to see the pyramids if you like. Millie, I'll do whatever you need. Please don't send me away again."

She remained quiet for a long moment, her lower lip drawn between her teeth. In his side vision, Ben could see her mother, the butler, the cook, and the footman all standing in the ballroom doorway.

Finally, Millie put a hand on each of the chair arms and pushed herself up. The chair moved slightly, and Ben grabbed her arms before she could fall, pulling her to her feet.

She wobbled for a moment then steadied herself, holding tightly to his arms. "I'll not have you remain out of guilt, Ben."

"It's not guilt, Millie. It's love. I love you."

"I love you too, Ben. I always have."

He slipped an arm around her waist and pulled her against him, cupping her face and kissing her just as he had when they were young. She hesitated at first, but her lips softened and she clung to him tightly.

Ben had thought he understood love as a boy pulling Millie's curls, or as a youth stealing a kiss by the pond, or even holding a small gold-covered box tied with a ribbon. But nothing compared to how he felt now, as a man holding the woman he loved, knowing she cared for him, she needed him. His broken heart knit back together and his soul felt whole.

He pulled back, holding her against him, her curls tickling his nose.

"Come. I know you're tired. You can sleep in the carriage."

"Where are we going?"

"Well, we are a few years late, but I believe we have an appointment. If we hurry, we can be to Gretna Green by morning. And if you'd like to invite your mother, I'm sure she'd be happy to come."

"But it is Christmas."

"Even better. I cannot think of a better Christmas gift."

Millie gave a smile so bright that the years of hurt, of loneliness and heartache, fell away, and Ben vowed to spend the rest of his life making sure neither of them hurt again.

ABOUT THE AUTHOR

JENNIFER MOORE LIVES WITH ONE husband and four sons, who produce heaps of laundry and laughter. She earned a BA from the University of Utah in linguistics, which she uses mostly for answering *Jeopardy* questions. A reader of history and romance, she loves traveling, tall ships, scented candles, and watching cake-decorating videos. When she's not driving carpool, writing, or helping with homework, she'll usually be found playing tennis. Learn more at authorjmoore.com and on Jennifer's social media.

Facebook: Author Jennifer Moore
Instagram: jennythebrave

OTHER BOOKS
BY KRISTA LYNNE JENSEN

Of Grace and Chocolate

The Orchard

Falling for You

Love Unexpected: With All My Heart (contributor)

Kisses in the Rain

Christmas at Canterwood

BY KRISTA LYNNE JENSEN

For my friends who told me I could, when life was telling me I couldn't. Merry Christmas.

CHAPTER 1

JULIA SEATON SMOOTHED HER SKIRTS and approached the table where the children had been practicing their letters. Algernon, the eldest of the Stanhope children, had graduated from ABCs years ago, but Sophia had been helping her younger sister, Helena, shape the G, *the most difficult of all the letters of the world*, as declared by little Helena with emphatic elocution. Julia smiled, picked up the sheets of paper, and hung them on the bit of clothesline she'd begged off Mrs. Nelson and fastened to the wall to display the children's best work.

The conquered G hung in prominence next to a pretty watercolor Sophia had painted of a fieldfare perched on a winter branch, and a map of the East Indies Algernon had copied from *Maps of the World*. He'd recently finished reading about Saint George and had insisted that the children playact his own interpretation. Julia had hesitated, unsure if playacting fell under acceptable forms of education in the Stanhope household. Mrs. Stanhope hadn't laid much in the way of boundaries in Julia's governessing. Quite the opposite—she'd left much to Julia's own discretion and expressed an abundance of faith in her children's new governess. Which—this being Julia's first position as a governess in a gentleman's home—left her in a constant state of either not overstepping boundaries or pushing the children's exploration of the world around them far enough.

As for herself, she leaned toward the latter.

And so the children had playacted Saint George slaying the dragon. They had been quite entertaining. Julia had gasped and applauded at all the right places.

And she had tried to keep the swashbuckling to a low clamor. Truly, she'd tried. Who would have guessed that dear Saint George was—in actuality—a pirate?

As if on cue, the airy noise of children's voices rose to the nursery window, and she crossed to the bright gray of a Northumberland December sky and drew the heavy lace curtain. More snow had come to Canterwood during the night. The light dusting was not enough to cancel the young thespians' riding lessons, and they'd paused to throw thin snowballs at one another on their way back to the house.

Julia laughed aloud and covered her mouth as Helena, half the size of her brother, rushed at him as he bent to form another snowball, and pushed her handfuls of snow onto his backside.

The little girl giggled as Alger stood quickly, rubbing his trousers and turning on her. She ran, squealing. Alger gave chase.

"Oh, Helena, watch your step," Julia muttered. But just as the little girl slipped on the icy stones, Alger caught her and spun them both around until they collapsed on the snow-packed lawn.

Grinning, Julia let the curtain fall and lifted her skirts as she hurried out of the nursery and down the staircase. She had better make sure the children got into the house before they tumbled in as giant snowballs.

But the children met her at the door, cheeks flushed and fingers pink from beneath their riding gloves.

"Oh, Miss Seaton," Helena sighed. "I wish I could stay out in the snow forever and never get cold."

Julia helped the child with her bonnet and coat. "And what would the rest of us do without you?"

"You would wave at me from the windows, and I would blow snowflake kisses at you."

Sophia laid her coat and gloves on top of Alger's things, which Nelson, the Stanhopes' butler, held patiently, waiting to take the clothes to be hung near a fire downstairs.

"You'd miss Betsy's hot chocolate," Sophia said. "And Alger would not be there to catch you if you slipped."

Helena pursed her rosy lips in thought. "Then I should come inside for just a little while. To have some chocolate. And anyhow, Alger slips as much as I do. Perhaps with enough practice I would be the one to catch him."

Alger shook his head. "Perhaps you should grow a few more inches before trying that."

Julia smiled. "Wise thinking." For Alger's eleven years, he could easily be mistaken for thirteen. She stood and laid the last of the coats on Nelson's arm. "Thank you, Nelson."

Nelson nodded in his very stately manner and left her to see that they all washed for tea. Then Julia shooed the slightly damp and chilled children into the drawing room, where a fire blazed in a marble fireplace as tall as Julia and wide enough to warm three children standing side to side.

"Who are these apple-cheeked children invading my drawing room?" Lady Teresa Stanhope peered around from her chair facing the fireplace.

"We've returned from our ride, Grandmama," Helena piped up.

"So I heard. And have you mastered the dappled pony?"

Helena sighed as Julia steered her to the hearth. "Not so well. He only wants to eat, and I don't know what to do about it. Sophia sits so well on Whisper, and Alger can jump Gilt as well as Papa."

"I certainly cannot," Alger protested.

"Well," Helena continued. "Nearly as well." She dropped her head and turned to the glow of the flames. "I can barely get Tulip to trot."

The others shared smiles over Helena's auburn head. It was no wonder the Stanhope children had so readily endeared themselves to Julia. Her position in this household was a blessing and eased the loneliness she'd been feeling as the holidays drew near; she was so far away from her own family.

Lady Teresa picked up her needlework. "You need to convince Tulip that trotting with you is a far more splendid thing than eating dry winter grass."

Helena turned. "But how do I do that?"

"Shall I tell you my secret?" Lady Teresa peered at Helena over her spectacles.

"Oh, please do!" Helena cried.

The older woman beckoned Helena closer and leaned forward, her eyes agleam with mischief. "Lemon drops."

Helena's eyes became round. "Lemon drops? Really, Grandmama?"

"It's worth a try, don't you think? But not too many. You don't want Tulip to get a bellyache."

Nodding solemnly, Helena turned back to the fire, holding out her hands for warmth. "It's worth a try," she repeated.

Lady Teresa winked at Alger, who winked back. Julia suspected this secret had been passed on before.

Taking tea in the drawing room with their grandmother had become a tradition the children didn't take lightly. Mr. Stanhope had taken his wife to visit her sister, who had recently brought a baby girl into the world. More specifically, into Yorkshire County. They'd been gone for three weeks. Being allowed tea in the drawing room after riding lessons was deemed a sort of compensation for being denied the presence of their parents, and the children had been promised that if they behaved as dignified little Stanhopes, the tradition would stand, even after their parents' return, as long as Lady Teresa wasn't receiving visitors.

And so they each sat in their favorite places, the children near their grandmama in front of the fire, and Julia taking the chair by the west window overlooking Betsy's dormant kitchen gardens, the greenhouse, and the neat rows of the orchard, every tree branch pillowed with snow.

Julia turned her head from the view outside. "Children, do you have a wreath for Christmas?"

Alger nodded. "Papa and I trim boughs for the staircase. Mama ties some into a big wreath for the front door."

"And then," Helena added, "Betsy makes plum pudding and we all make wishes. Mama always goes first." She bit into her biscuit. "I do hope they get home in time."

"Don't talk with your mouth full, Helena," Lady Teresa said.

"Sorry, Grandmama," Helena said, her mouth still full.

Julia stifled a laugh.

Sophia set her cup in its saucer and her shoulders sloped. "I miss Mama."

Julia straightened. "Of course you do, darling. But they'll be home soon, isn't that right, Lady Teresa? Nothing has changed, I hope?"

"You are right, Miss Seaton. Sophia, my dear, your mother's last letter promised they'll be home before Christmas Eve, and they'll be so happy to see you all. And to be out of that carriage, no doubt."

Sophia nodded. She had taken the absence of her parents particularly hard. She was not a moping child, but rather a deep thinker, and Julia believed Sophia placed a great deal of her own feelings of safety and assurance on the presence of her mama, as any deep-thinking, deep-feeling nine-year-old would do.

An idea formed, and Julia set down her empty teacup. "I know what we'll do. We'll go upstairs and plan your parents' Christmas presents."

Helena nearly upset the tea tray as she stood from her little stool and bounced toward Julia. Her grandmama steadied the tray. "May we make our presents?" Helena asked.

"Of course you may."

Sophia stood as well, though more carefully. "What will we make?" she asked.

Julia was pleased to see a spark in Sophia's eyes. "Well, why don't the three of you go upstairs to the nursery and start thinking. I'll be up shortly."

"Excellent idea," Lady Teresa said. "I'm expecting the vicar to come by at any moment, and I'd prefer to have a quiet chat with him."

"I'll just leave with the children, then, ma'am." Before Julia could bob a curtsy, Lady Teresa held up her hand.

"I'd like you to stay, if you please, Miss Seaton. There's a small matter I'd like your opinion on."

Julia did bob a curtsy then, and sat back down as the children kissed their grandmama and tumbled out of the room and up the stairs already offering ideas for Christmas presents. She heard the words "ruby-crusted umbrella stand" and "a real elephant to ride" but thought—or hoped—she was wrong. Anyhow, her thoughts were no longer on presents but on the fact that the vicar was coming by and she'd been asked to stay.

She popped up from her seat again, crossed to where the remains of the children's tea waited as if biscuits had done battle with spoons, and began to tidy up.

"Julia, we have people for that. Nessa will be in shortly."

Julia left the dishes and stepped to the fireplace, avoiding Lady Teresa's intent gaze. One of the things she loved about the old woman was that when no one else was around, she addressed Julia by her given name, just as her mother had done. It had made her feel more at ease in those first unnerving weeks here, and still did. She was *Miss Seaton* in front of the children to set a precedent and *Julia* when the children were gone—as Lady Teresa had said, "To help you remember who you truly are."

"Why did you wish me to remain, Lady Teresa? Surely you don't need my help entertaining the vicar?" She smiled and glanced at the woman. Sitting like this in the afternoon light, in the glow of the fire, Lady Teresa looked much less grandmotherly and more like the beautiful socialite Julia had heard stories about from her own mother before she came here—the daughter of an earl, who had married a gentleman horseman. She'd removed her spectacles and her gray-blue eyes danced in the reflecting fire. Julia had never seen her wear a large, frilly mobcap as some women her age, but instead a neat lace wrap, her gray-blonde hair loosely pinned in curls underneath. Her gowns were always silk, and her posture was always perfect. Julia stood a little straighter.

"You yourself said you should stay when you sent the children above. Did you have something you wished to ask me?" Lady Teresa looked at her expectantly.

"Oh, well, it was nothing important." Julia clasped her hands in front of her. Nessa appeared to take away the tea things. "I only wondered what would happen if . . ." She glanced toward the door as Nessa exited, and lowered her voice. "If the Stanhopes do not return in time for the children to begin their Christmas traditions."

"My thoughts exactly, Julia. Ophelia's promise that they will be home before Christmas Eve leaves me to wonder if they will be home days before Christmas Eve, or minutes. I think we must hope for the former and depend upon the latter. I'll talk to James about procuring boughs. And goodness, I've never tied a wreath. Perhaps . . .?"

"I will make the attempt," Julia answered. "I've tied herbs for drying, and bouquets of spring flowers. It can't be much different than that."

"Oh, bless you. I've no idea when Betsy starts her pudding. I'll talk to her and see what must be done about this stirring and wishing."

Julia smiled. "Do you not stir and wish, ma'am?"

"Oh, as a very small child. Some of our English traditions were mislaid during our time in the West Indies, and Charles never cared for plum pudding, I'm afraid. I've been remiss and shall make amends."

Just then, the door opened and Nelson entered. "Mr. Langley here to see you, Lady Teresa."

She rose. "Do show him in. Julia, don't fidget."

Julia stilled her fingers on her dress. She didn't know why the vicar made her want to stare at the wall or worry her fingers behind her back. He was a young vicar, the youngest son of an upstanding family who lived nearby, Lady Teresa had told her. His father was the steward of an earl or something of that nature. And though he was handsome, with his neat brown hair and wide brown eyes and the square cut of his chin, he was so very serious to the point of being solemn. She had never seen him smile. During his last sermon, Julia had decided against him being stern. He was not that, at least. But he was solemn, and she did not know what to do with solemn people. Especially one so close to her age. So she fidgeted.

The vicar appeared at the door.

"Mr. Langley, do sit down. You know our governess, Miss Seaton?"

"Yes, of course." He removed his vicar's hat and bowed. "Good afternoon."

Julia lowered her eyes and curtsied. "Good afternoon, Mr. Langley. I hope you are well?"

He didn't quite meet Julia's gaze. "Yes, thank you."

He waited until the women were seated and then took the seat Lady Stanhope offered him.

"Thank you for coming, Thomas. I do hope your mother is well?"

He bowed his head. "Yes, she is fully recovered."

"Was she very ill?" Julia asked.

He turned his head toward her, but still his gaze was somewhere about her chair leg. "Not very ill. A sore throat. But she is better. They left this morning to visit my brother in Devonshire for the holiday."

"I'm glad to hear it," Julia said. "That your mother is well, I mean." She squeezed her hands in her lap and looked at the fire, remembering her father's illness. It had come so quickly.

When she turned back, she met the vicar's solemn but direct gaze. Soft brown eyes beneath severe dark brows. But they weren't severe, only . . . considering. They lifted, and he turned away, blinking.

"Lady Teresa," he said, "you mentioned you had some items for the less fortunate?"

"I do. Nelson will bring the basket when you leave. Some shawls and blankets, stockings, and bundles of Betsy's rich molasses cakes."

"With currants and apples," he said.

"I can assure you they are the very same."

"Excellent. God bless you and this home, dear Lady. Have you word of Richard?"

"Not since October, but we're hoping with the defeat of that French— menace—he will be home soon."

Richard Stanhope was Lady Teresa's younger son, away fighting Napoleon's army as so many of their men were.

"You know Mr. Stanhope?" Julia asked. Lady Teresa rarely mentioned him, only when a letter came, and she was still private about that, even with governesses she addressed by Christian name.

"He is my good friend, Miss Seaton," the vicar said. "We were boys together, and when it was time to become men, I chose the church and he, being the fine horseman that he is, chose the cavalry." He turned to Lady Teresa and rested his hand upon hers. "There are always several months between letters, are there not?"

Lady Teresa grasped his hand. "Yes. And just when my hope begins to waver, a letter comes, and it's as if he was just here."

"Hold on to your hope. The war is ending. You'll hear from him."

Lady Teresa nodded, her shoulders straight. But Julia observed the slight quiver of her chin.

"It is the season of miracles," the vicar said in his solemn way, his brown eyes soft.

"It is, Thomas," Lady Teresa said. "It is." She let go of his hand and pulled a handkerchief from her sleeve. Dabbing at her eyes, she became herself again. "Which reminds me. Julia—Miss Seaton—and I have been discussing the return of my eldest son and his wife from Yorkshire. The hope is that they will arrive before Christmas Eve, but we are unsure of how soon that will be. I hope it isn't too imperious of me to ask, but do you think you could come up with some good work of some sort to keep the children preoccupied for a morning or afternoon? Not something frivolous like a sleigh ride or caroling, but perhaps filling a need in the parish—mind you their safety—to take their minds off themselves and broaden their views of the world, if you will?"

Julia sat up. "What a good idea. Something that matters."

"Yes, exactly, my dear. Something that matters. Do you have any thoughts?"

"Well, no, not specifically." Julia looked at Mr. Langley.

"I've no ideas at the moment," he said. "But there is always a need."

"I'm sure the two of you can put your heads together and come up with something." Lady Teresa made to stand, but Julia reached out and held her arm.

"Heads? Together?" She didn't dare glance at the vicar, and she was keenly aware that he was trying very hard not to look at her.

"Certainly. How do you expect to come up with a plan if you do not communicate?" Lady Teresa stood, and Mr. Langley just after. "I'm going to pop into the kitchen and talk to Cook," she said.

"But the children," Julia said. "They're waiting for me."

Without a glance back at either of them, Lady Teresa fluttered her fingers in the air. "Oh, let them be children for a few minutes."

And with that, Julia and the vicar were left alone in the drawing room. At least the woman had the decency to leave the door open.

Julia stood. The vicar gripped his hat in his fingers. He turned it around a full rotation before she decided he was not going to begin.

"Well," she said, perhaps a little too brightly, "what are some needs of the parish that could be met by . . . a five-, nine-, and eleven-year-old child?"

He turned, frowning in thought, and walked to the window where she'd been sitting earlier. He brought his hat behind his back and clasped it there with both hands. "We have a soup lunch on Christmas Eve, but I believe we're meant to think of something between now and then."

"That gives us four days."

"Three, not counting the Sabbath," he said.

"Oh, yes, of course. Do you need vegetables prepared for the soup? Ingredients gathered?"

"Hmm," was the only sound he made.

"Wood chopped for the fire?" she added.

He turned to her. "I have enough wood chopped for all of winter, thank you, Miss Seaton."

"What about the less fortunate? Do they have wood chopped for all of winter?"

He tilted his head and studied her. "So far, everything you've suggested involves a sharp blade. Is that wise?"

She could imagine Sophia using a smaller knife to help cut up carrots and potatoes, but not Helena. And the sudden image of Alger with his play swords came to mind. "Perhaps not."

"Hmm." He went back to frowning and looking out the window. "I pay the older children of families in need to gather up items for the meal. And the farmers' wives have had the entire thing running smoothly far longer than I've been here. But you know . . ." He turned suddenly. "It would be something to give the families an extra bundle of wood."

"For Christmas day," she said. "Maybe longer. A week." She watched him pace and then stopped watching him because she feared she was watching him too much. One shouldn't watch a vicar too much. "Could we use some of the wood from the vicarage?" she asked.

He paused and looked out the window. He spoke softly. "We have thirty families expected for that lunch."

"So many?" she asked, stepping up beside him at the window.

He nodded. "And more that cannot make the lunch because they are ill or elderly."

"Well then, perhaps the vicarage doesn't need wood for *all* of winter."

"I assure you, Miss Seaton, my summation takes into account that it is only I who would be in need of warmth and the congregants on Sundays."

Her fingers wrung. "Of course. I didn't mean to imply that you were greedy, by any means. I was . . . joking. My father would say, 'Cold church, cross parishioners.'"

The corner of his mouth twitched. "Your father was an observant man. But you're right, the vicarage doesn't need wood for all of winter. I could go into the trees and chop more, I suppose."

They stood quietly at the window.

"It seems like so little," Julia said. "A bundle of wood."

"Yes it does. Perhaps," he said, with a small tilt of his head, "the Stanhopes wouldn't notice if one of their apple trees went missing."

Julia pressed her fingers over her mouth, smothering her smile. She detected a trace of humor in his eyes as he looked out over the orchard. "I am glad you're joking," she said.

"Who says I'm joking?"

She pressed her lips together, dropping her eyes to the windowsill, and allowed a smile to surface. Daring a glance up, she found him watching her.

She quickly looked out the window again. Then sighed. "I almost wish you weren't joking. A part of me wishes to chop one down myself if it meant a larger ration for everyone. The children were so cold earlier when they came inside from the snow, but happily so. And look what they had to stand in front of." She gestured to the grand fireplace.

He looked toward the fireplace but said nothing. The snap and pop of the burning logs were the only sounds to fill the silence.

Finally, the vicar leaned against the window frame. "Can you think of no alternative to theft?"

She didn't know what to think of him, standing here at this tall window with her, looking out over a small orchard and contemplating stealing a tree.

"I'm afraid we must find an alternative," she said. "The eighth commandment is quite clear on the subject."

She spied him silently counting on his fingers.

Again, she looked quickly out the window, her eyes wide. Was he playing?

A low, quiet chuckle let her know he was. Truly, this was a side of Mr. Langley she'd never seen before.

As moments passed, the vastness of the Stanhopes' estate touched her. Fields of horse pasture, training arenas, and the stables, a walking garden, and yes, a wild copse of forest in addition to the orchard and the vegetable and herb gardens.

She turned to the vicar with an idea. "Mr. Langley, we could ask those who have an abundance to donate," she said. "If we could get only ten parishioners to donate a bundle of wood, or even coal, that's a third of the battle. I'm sure the Stanhopes could donate three or four bundles and—unlike an entire tree—it wouldn't even be missed."

His brow lifted.

She slowly closed her eyes as she felt her face warm up. "Forgive me. That was terribly presumptuous."

"It was. But it was also true."

Her eyes opened, and she found the vicar smiling. Half-smiling. A magical half-smile.

"Oh, heavens," she whispered.

He leaned toward her. "Pardon me?"

"No. Just"—she swallowed—"I shouldn't have said that. About the Stanhopes."

"It hardly falls under the tenth commandment, Miss Seaton."

"The tenth?"

He lowered his voice. "Coveting what is thy neighbor's."

"Oh, yes, of course," she managed in little more than a whisper. "The tenth."

He straightened; his smile vanished. "Do not fret. I can say the same thing of my home. This is a good start. If we can get the wood collected from wherever the Lord directs us, we can help the children tie up the bundles—"

"With red ribbons," she proposed.

"—with red ribbons, and distribute them after the luncheon. Will you . . ." he grew solemn again. "Will you pray with me, Miss Stanhope?"

Julia blinked at the request but quickly recovered. "Yes, of course. Right here?"

He glanced around. "The Stanhopes have not added a chapel to their estate in recent months?"

She shook her head.

"Then right here will do."

She nodded and bowed her head as he did.

As he petitioned the Lord for direction and success with the children and for ways truly to help those in need this season and always, it occurred to her that he had been teasing her about the chapel.

CHAPTER 2

GRATEFUL THE SNOW HADN'T FALLEN too heavily, Thomas Langley pulled his bay to a standstill and looked behind him. Canterwood had been singularly important to him as a boy. It had always held as much of a welcome to him as—if not more than—his parents' home when he'd returned from Eton and then Cambridge. And yet he'd never felt it so changed as upon this visit.

With old Mr. Stanhope gone from this world, and Frank and Ophelia away for nearly a month, he felt the absence of his friend Richard most profoundly. He missed him, and he worried about him. His own letter from Richard was five months old, and likely a more dismal account of the atrocities of war than Lady Stanhope's. Which was as it should be. But the brutal picture Richard had painted frustrated Thomas. His first inclination, as it always had been, was to help. To be at Richard's side and defeat the foe. To bring an end to this awful war and bring everyone home, safe and sound.

But he wasn't there. He was needed here, his mother liked to remind him. At least, he was working to be needed here. And lately, nothing felt like it was enough.

His shoulders fell. That wasn't true. He'd grown to love his work, and he was grateful to have been given this living so near the place where he'd grown up. His eyes had been opened to how much he'd had and how seldom he'd thought of it. He was blessed, and now he said a silent prayer for Richard and those in need of greater blessings than himself.

A snowflake fell against his cheek, and he blinked. As he noticed the new falling snow, lights flickered on in the upstairs room of the house. The nursery. The old lace curtain at one of the windows drew aside, and Miss Seaton stood there with little Helena, watching the snow. The little girl hopped up and down and then spied him.

Thomas straightened in the saddle as the little girl waved, and then Miss Seaton found him. She too waved. His lungs filled with winter air, and he lifted a hand and waved back. He thought he saw her smile, but the light was behind her and the sun setting. Good sense told him to get moving, but he waited as the girls stepped away and closed the curtain.

Renewed, he urged his horse forward, and found himself reliving Miss Seaton's smile. The small dimple on her right cheek and the light in her hazel eyes. He'd made a fool of himself attempting to make her smile again and again. Perhaps not *such* a fool, as he'd met with some success.

But Thomas chastised himself for losing his focus with Miss Seaton. If only Lady Teresa had stayed as chaperone. What had she been thinking, leaving him there with the young woman, alone? He knew what she was thinking— that the local vicar could be trusted with her family governess.

And of course, he could be. He knew little of Miss Seaton but that she came from a genteel family who had recently lost their father. And so, it was only the work of compassion to coax a smile from her, was it not? Even if he made shoddy work of it?

And what was it to him if her light-brown hair curled just so at her temples and the nape of her neck? Or if the yellow of her gown set off the rose of her cheeks?

Nothing at all.

Except that he was having such a difficult time focusing now that he'd missed the lane back to the vicarage. What would Richard say? Hmm, never mind what Richard would say.

A second reason for Lady Teresa's quick departure from the drawing room suddenly hit him broadside. But he shoved it away, feeling his cheeks warm with chagrin.

He had determined long ago not to marry young. After seeing school chums quickly enter matrimony and then find themselves "trapped" in a marriage they no longer wanted, with a poor wife they no longer valued, he'd promised himself he would not do that to a trusting girl. Let alone himself.

He took a deep breath. He would be vicar. He would build his own foundation of character and home and maturity while fulfilling his call before he dared offer any of it to a woman like Miss Julia Seaton. Or any other person, he quickly added. Years from now.

He would see Miss Seaton—the family—tomorrow at church. He could start afresh then. Lady Teresa had asked for a service endeavor for the children. That's what she would get. No more.

～✑～

Julia stepped back from the nursery window, her face warm despite the draft.

"I would like to have seen the vicar," Helena said. "He tries not to smile, but sometimes he can't help it, I think. Especially when I do this." Helena crossed her eyes and stuck out her tongue.

"Helena!" Julia cried out, choking down laughter. "When do you make that face at the poor vicar?"

"During his sermon. But don't worry, I wait until the less important parts."

Julia groaned. "You must not make that face at the vicar—or anybody—ever again. Is that understood?"

Helena's gaze dropped to the floor. "I was just trying to help."

"Well, I have another way you can help. One that doesn't involve making the vicar laugh during his sermons. He works hard on those and practices so that all the parts are important."

Helena nodded, and Julia was somewhat assured.

"What other way?" the little girl asked.

"Well." She motioned for the older children to come sit at the table. "We're going to put together great bundles of firewood and coal for those who are especially cold in the winter. And we'll help with the Christmas Eve luncheon at the church. What do you think of that?"

"Will I get to chop the wood?" Alger asked.

"Hmm, we'll have to talk to Mr. Langley about that, but perhaps."

"Will we give wood to the Daceys?" Sophia asked quietly.

Julia took her own seat at the table. "Who are the Daceys, darling?"

"When Mama and I take bread to Furrows Street, we visit the Daceys. They have seven children, and one, Eliza, is my age. Eliza said her papa and eldest brother are at the war. Their house is awfully small and cold, and they have two babies. May we give her some firewood?"

Julia reached for her hand. "Of course we may."

"I'm certain *that* would make Mr. Langley smile," Helena said, pulling her doll, Lucy-Anne, onto her lap.

Julia remembered his elusive smile and the remarkable flip of her insides because of it. "I hope you're right, Helena." After letting her gaze wander for a moment or two in the direction Mr. Langley had ridden off on his horse, Julia straightened in her chair. "Now, what have you come up with for your Christmas presents? Sophia? What are you working on?"

"I've decided to paint a picture of Canterwood."

"What a clever idea. Shall you have it covered in snow?"

Sophia giggled. "No. I shall have it in summer, with ivy clambering up and the beech trees all in splendor."

"I have not seen them in their green. They wore russet when I arrived. I look forward to your likeness."

The girl beamed.

"Helena? What are your ideas?"

Helena slid her head to her folded arms quite dramatically. "I do not know." She sighed. "Either a seashell box for Mama and a muslin bread pouch for Papa for when he takes me to feed the ducks, or a peacock feather for Mama's hair and an abalone cravat pin for Papa."

Julia lifted her brow. "Do you have a peacock feather?"

"No, but I imagined I would happen upon one, if I could ever get Tulip to take me farther than the paddock."

"Hmm. I see your dilemma. Peacock feathers are immensely difficult to happen upon in paddocks . . . in December. And the abalone pin?"

Helena raised her gaze to Julia's. "I have a bit of abalone in my seashell collection. So all I need is a pin."

"Well, that is something. They are all superb ideas. Let's think on it some more, shall we?"

Helena nodded.

"And you, Alger? What have you been conjuring up for your parents?"

Alger sat up straighter in his chair. He had recently been given his own bedroom, and everything in the nursery seemed too small for him. "I would like to give them a play."

Julia's eyebrows shot nearly to the ceiling. "A play?" Not wanting to sound discouraging, and unsure as to whether or not she should be dismayed, she softened her voice. "What type of play?"

Alger laughed, shaking his head. "A Christmas play, Miss Seaton. Of course."

"Of course," she said. "But . . . what type of Christmas play?" She pictured highway robbers, pirates, and gypsies.

"The Christmas play. You know, Mother Mary and taxation and the stable all forlorn. *That* Christmas play." He folded his arms, looking very proud of himself.

Helena leapt from her chair, crashing into her brother's shoulder. "Oh, that is a marvelous idea, Alger. May I be in it?"

"And I?" Sophia asked.

"Of course. I'll need all of you. And you, Miss Seaton."

"Me?" Julia felt her hold on her flock of ducklings slipping, and fast. "I'm not sure—"

"And a few others, of course. I've written down all of the parts, and we can double up on some if they don't appear simultaneously on stage."

"Stage?" asked Julia.

"Of course," Alger said, looking at her as if she were daft. "There will have to be a place set apart where the action takes place."

"Well, won't the nursery do as always? We can move the table—"

Alger stood and folded his arms, surveying the now very diminutive nursery. "I don't think so. Not for this play. This play is special."

Julia couldn't argue with that. But all of her societal instinct and upbringing warned her that this would not do. Outside of a nursery the play, the theatre, the baseness of such performance could either be welcome and taken with heart . . . or it could be very much frowned upon, and not only might the children be reprimanded, it might even cost her this position.

"Perhaps in the library?" she thought aloud. All the books dampened sound in there.

"Or the drawing room!" Alger's enthusiasm would not be contained. Apparently, not even to the library.

"Oh, dear."

Alger sat down. "Do you not think it a good idea, Miss Seaton?"

"I . . ." She watched the sincerity, the hope, the good heart of her charge sink as he began to question himself. "I do wonder if you would write it out for me, Alger, and then we could decide if . . ." Oh, how could she word this. ". . . if the subject of the story would find it acceptable."

He frowned. "The subject of the story?"

"Yes," she said gently. "Our Lord, Jesus?"

He broke out into a smile and lifted his chin. "Oh, of course. Excellent idea, Miss Seaton. I shall keep that in mind while I write it." His frown returned. "That's a bit of pressure, isn't it, Miss Seaton?"

Not so much pressure as I will feel proposing we turn Lady Teresa's drawing room into a miniature Bethlehem, Julia thought.

"It's quite a responsibility, Alger." She rested her hand on his shoulder. "I know you'll do your best."

He nodded, biting his lip, already lost in the workings of his thoughts.

"May I be Mary?" Helena asked. She cradled Lucy-Anne in her arms as if to practice.

Alger held up his hand, pulling over some paper and taking up a pencil. "I need to think about it," he said and began writing in deep concentration.

As Helena began to open her mouth again, Julia intervened.

"Why don't we sort through your seashell collection, Helena?"

As she rose to follow Helena to the cupboards, she glanced around and knew that the boy's imagination would not confine this particular play to the nursery. She closed her eyes and sighed then opened them again at the loud crash that was Helena's seashell collection, now spilled on the floor, where the bottom of the old hat box had given way.

Helena looked up guiltily at Julia.

"Some of these would look lovely pasted on a sturdy glove box I was just going to throw out," Julia said. "Your mother could use it on her desk however she likes. What do you think?"

The little girl nodded, and smiled. "That would be lovely, Miss Seaton."

CHAPTER 3

After church, Julia waited near the Stanhope carriage with the children while Lady Teresa finished visiting with friends. The snow had stopped during the night, and the day had proven unusually bright, though chilly. The house staff had already left to walk home. Watching them, she had felt the compulsion to knit them all new mufflers for Christmas and wished she'd thought of it sooner. She wondered what they would think of a gift at all. Though they were polite to her, Julia didn't know where she stood with them. She was neither belowstairs nor a houseguest, and certainly was not family. A quiet girl, Tilde, helped her dress in the mornings and made sure her clothes were fresh and put away, but Julia always had to squelch the urge to help her. She'd attempted to do so when she'd first arrived and the girl had been near to tears. So she was waited on but didn't feel as though she should be, and was not invited to dine with the staff, but could not dine with the family. She either took her meals with the children or alone in her room. Her mother had warned her that a governess could be a lonely position. Julia hadn't understood what she'd meant at the time. She hoped it would not grow to be too terrible.

Julia decided she would knit Tilde a muffler. A soft violet.

She spied the vicar shaking hands with the Carringtons in farewell and could not help but notice now how he seemed to care very much about his parishioners, no matter how little he smiled. After their interaction yesterday, a lot of her opinions of the vicar had changed. He wasn't dismal; he was compassionate. He wasn't serious; he was concerned. He was . . . now in conversation with Alger.

Oh dear.

Julia took Helena's hand and hurried, Sophia following, to intercede.

Mr. Langley looked up at her approach, his expression concerned. Quite concerned.

Alger was animated. "And so I asked myself, right in the middle of your sermon, 'Who better to ask for direction of a Christmas play than a man of God?' Would you help me, sir? I would be so grateful."

"Oh yes, Vicar," said Helena, her restraint showing in only a slight bounce on her toes. "I think that should make you smile very much."

Julia felt her ears redden, and not from the cold. "Children, I don't think we should bother the vicar."

Mr. Langley rested his hand on Alger's shoulder. "May I have a word with Miss Seaton, Algernon?"

Alger nodded.

"Children," she said, "go ask James if you can give the horses a carrot. I know he has some."

The children ran off.

She turned back to the vicar. "Mr. Langley, I'm terribly sorry—"

"Are you actually encouraging the children in this business of a play?"

Julia paused, hearing his tone. It was not a tone of compassion. And his soft brown eyes were now tinged with accusation. Her chin came up. "Yes. Yes, I am."

"Have you spoken to their grandmother of it?"

"Well, no. I haven't. I meant to, but the children begged me not to. It's meant to be a surprise for their parents as well as Lady Teresa." Julia glanced toward the woman and lowered her voice. "As a Christmas gift."

He glanced that direction and lowered his voice as well. "Did you consider the propriety of such an idea? The reverenced and hallowed account of the birth of our Lord in the hands of a child? Is this something that was acceptable in your parents' home?"

She flinched and stepped back. "You believe this to be my idea?"

He nodded. "Of course."

She straightened her shoulders and fought to keep her voice low. "The play is Algernon's idea, from beginning to end. But I'll have you know that even if it were my idea, what matters is Alger. He had his nose buried in the book of Luke this morning, taking notes. He is determined to treat the subject with all the respect an eleven-year-old boy can muster and then some. If he weren't, he would not have dared come ask you for help."

"Miss Seaton—"

She wasn't finished. "And as for what was *acceptable* in my parents' home, we were encouraged to learn. From the best books. And to apply what we learned to the world around us, no matter how small that world may have been. Be that through poetry or paint or mathematics or music or yes, even playacting. Because we were *children*, Mr. Langley. And my father, God rest his soul, believed that of such were the kingdom of *heaven*."

Her breath came fast and she blinked rapidly, her indignation mixed with discomfiture. She turned away, taking a deep breath to compose herself. Oh, she shouldn't have lost her temper like that. Too late now. She'd meant every word, but why did it sting so?

"Miss Seaton?"

He'd spoken her name softly. She closed her eyes and debated whether to turn around or not.

"I apologize, Miss Seaton. Deeply. I did not, nor would I ever, mean to insult you or your family. It was very wrong of me."

She dropped her head and nodded.

"Guide me in how I may earn your forgiveness," he said quietly.

She looked back and met his earnest gaze. He held his hat in his hands, looking in every way contrite. Very well, then. She straightened. "You can help Alger with this play."

The corner of his mouth twitched upward, giving her hope, and he hung his head. He replaced his hat and once more lifted his gaze to hers in a way that made her breath catch.

"You have won then, Miss Seaton. And rightly so."

A smile grew, one that did not stop at her mouth. "You'll help us, then? I mean, Alger? You'll help make this play a decent and noble thing?"

He gave her a slow nod.

"And you'll remember that they are just children wanting to do a bit of good?"

Again, he fought a smile. "I was a child once. Sometimes I forget."

"Then, Mr. Langley, I'll consider forgiving you."

A look of relief brushed across his face. He bowed his head. "I'll call on you—all of you—in the morning. Ten o'clock. We are taking the children around to beg firewood. First beggars, then actors. Frank will have my skin."

"If he's to have anyone's skin, I'm sure it will be mine. I fear my position may be in danger."

"Not if you state your case to him the way you did to me just now." He studied her for a moment. "Assure Alger that I'll be ready to answer his questions as best I can."

Julia curtsied, heady with triumph. "Thank you, Vicar."

He bowed low.

They both turned as Lady Teresa approached.

"Are you two sufficiently frozen yet?" she asked.

"Not quite," Julia said. "We were discussing your assignment." Among other things.

"Excellent. I'm sure you'll both make this a Christmas the children won't forget. Good day to you, Thomas. I'm going home to thaw. Miss Seaton?" Lady Teresa left for the carriage.

Julia eyed the vicar, who peered back at her. "Good day, Mr. Langley," she said.

"Good day," he said, his gaze direct.

Finally, she turned and followed Lady Teresa, her boots crunching on the gravel and snow.

"Miss Seaton?"

She turned back to the vicar.

"Your father . . ." he said. "He was a lawyer, then?"

"No," she said with a grin, emotion welling in her throat. "A vicar."

He watched her, motionless, and she turned and alighted the steps to the carriage, the children beaming at her inside.

CHAPTER 4

WHEN THOMAS ARRIVED ON HORSEBACK the following morning, making the trip through twenty inches of new snow on top of what had already been packed down, he had expected to deliver bad news that their firewood collecting would have to wait until the roads were more serviceable. But Lady Teresa had declared this nonsense and put James to work readying the sleigh and adding to that a pile of cut firewood and four buckets of coal.

"People are apt to give more when they've seen that others have given as well," she had said with a trace of a wink, a credit to that Lady's shrewd mind, and reminding him of Richard.

The little girls were bundled up and piled under blankets on a low bench in the back, excitement gleaming in their faces, but not so much as what Thomas saw in Miss Seaton. He ignored the dig of disappointment in his chest when Algernon took the seat on the bench next to him, Miss Seaton sitting on the end. Of course, that was most proper; and of course, Alger would use this opportunity to discuss his play; and of course, Thomas should not have been bothered by it in the first place. He had not come to court Miss Seaton. And he pushed away the infernal idea blossoming in his head of coming for that purpose another time.

"Is everything all right, Mr. Langley?"

He looked over at her, her golden eyes alight, the hood of her brown cloak not entirely concealing a stray curl resting against her rosy cheek, the wintry air gently stirring the bits of snow floating around them.

He blinked and looked away. "Nothing. I mean—yes, are we ready to go?"

Before she could respond, he prodded the pretty team James had hitched up onto the drive, and with a lurch, they were off, gliding through the snow.

"Do you think Papa and Mama have left our aunt's house yet?" Alger asked between them, taking in the surrounding white.

"Perhaps," Miss Seaton answered. "Your father is well aware of the distance of the journey and of the . . ." she paused as if searching for the correct word, "*challenges* the weather can pose this time of year. I'm sure he's taking that into careful consideration."

Thomas glanced over the boy's head and caught Miss Seaton's eye.

"And don't forget," he added. "Your mama will be eager to get home to you children. Though I can't for the life of me figure why." He raised an eyebrow at Alger, and the boy grinned and ducked his head.

"Mr. Langley, don't you think we're good children?" asked Helena from behind him.

"I think Mr. Langley was teasing you, darling," Miss Seaton said. "At least I hope so."

Thomas kept his gaze ahead on the horses, fighting his own grin. "Vicars don't tease," he said. "It's a fact."

"I have personal experience to the contrary, Mr. Langley," she countered. "It so happens my father teased us terribly."

The children giggled.

Of course. He'd forgotten that little unveiling from yesterday. It had kept him pacing in front of his hearth for some time afterward. "Tell me then, in what ways did your father tease you?"

He watched her set her hands in her lap and her gaze drift. "Oh . . ." She smiled and that dazzling dimple appeared. "Sometimes he would call our names early in the morning, knowing we would rush to dress and hurry downstairs. And you know? He'd tied all our bootlaces together—sometimes not even a matched pair. To my shame, I always fell for that. Or"—she continued through the children's laughter— "once, I had been allowed to buy a cluster of silk flowers and a feather or two for a new bonnet, and perhaps I had spent a little too much time primping and poking that thing. And Sunday morning before he left, my father stuck a pinecone right there in the silk flowers, and I didn't notice until after church when Clara DeLong came up to me and said straight out, 'Julia, I would never have thought to stick a pinecone on my bonnet. You are bold.' I'm sure I turned as red as a beet."

"Do young ladies not wear pinecones on their bonnets?" Thomas asked, straight-faced.

"No, they do not," she said, laughing. "Berries and feathers, and perhaps even a pretty spray of twigs, but not big fat *pinecones*."

He chuckled. "Well, then. I'm proved wrong once more. Children, beware—vicars do tease."

Miss Seaton's laughter died down, and her eyes glistened. But her smile widened.

"Mr. Langley, you're smiling," Helena said. "Doesn't he have a nice smile, Miss Seaton? Vicars can have nice smiles, can't they?"

Thomas cleared his throat and moved his attention to the horses, but he felt Miss Seaton's gaze still upon him.

"Indeed they can, Helena," she said. "Even when they try not to have them."

Thomas couldn't help but feel relief when they pulled up to the Carringtons' home. He jumped down quickly to help the little girls, noting that Alger had hurried to give Miss Seaton a hand down even before the footman could get to her. Good lad.

They made their way up the cleared steps to the door and were let inside, enveloped in warmth. Mrs. Carrington soon greeted them.

"Well, isn't this a fine-looking group?" she asked. "Vicar, Miss Seaton, welcome." She bent down to Sophia's level. "What can I help you with, children?"

Sophia tucked her chin in, likely shy of being singled out. He'd noticed that of her, being a middle child himself, that she was far less forward than her siblings. Still, she spoke with conviction, and that surprised him.

"Please, ma'am, we are collecting firewood for our friends who might not be warm enough for Christmas."

"Your friends?" the woman asked, her brows high.

Sophia pressed on. "Yes, ma'am. The Daceys and the Prices and the Binfords and so on."

Thomas smiled. How had this little girl of privilege learned to reach beyond her status to make such friends?

"Well now, I've always thought it best to be warm at Christmas. Mr. Carrington and I will be happy to help."

Sophia's eyes widened as she looked up at Miss Seaton in surprise.

"What do you say, children?" Miss Seaton asked.

After a small chorus of thank-yous and a tray of cookies had passed around, Mrs. Carrington took Thomas aside.

"Matthew is loading the firewood onto your sleigh this very minute. Is there anything else we can help you with?"

"You are too kind. We'll not press any more upon your generosity."

"You'll let us know if you need anything else?" She looked at the children fondly. "I do hope their parents arrive home in time. Children go with Christmas like jam with bread."

Thomas studied the children, considering her words.

After they had all piled into the sleigh again, he caught Miss Seaton eyeing him suspiciously.

"You have something to say to me, Miss Seaton?" he asked. He urged the horses forward.

"Did Mrs. Carrington know we were coming?"

"Yes. I mentioned it to her on Sunday."

She nodded and said no more.

"Mr. Langley," Alger said. "About the Christmas play."

Thomas readied a look of grave contemplation, which should have been easier for a vicar. "Yes, the play. I understand you are keeping it traditional."

"I'm trying, sir. But I'm not certain where to begin the story. Do we start with the angel Gabriel visiting Elizabeth and then Mary, and the babes leaping in their wombs and all of that?" Out of the corner of his eye, Thomas observed Miss Seaton's mouth dropping into a perfect 'O'. "Or do we begin with the decree by Caesar Augustus that all shall be taxed? And skip John the Baptist? Because his part is all rather exciting, isn't it?"

"I see your dilemma," Thomas answered, having to clear his throat with a small cough so as not to laugh as Miss Seaton put her hand over her eyes. "Traditionally, the story of Christmas begins with the decree by Caesar Augustus. It is, after all, the story of the *birth* of our Savior, not the story of Mary's, uh, confinement. As blessed and noble as that portion is."

"I was afraid of that," Alger said, clearly dejected. "I really liked all of the angel parts."

"Yes, well, one can never have too many angel parts. But there are several angel parts as the story continues."

"That is true," said Alger, his brows furrowed in consideration. "Poor John gets a bit overshadowed by his cousin, doesn't he?"

"He does. But he doesn't mind."

"Ever?"

"Not ever. Trust me on this, Alger."

"All right, then." He leaned forward with his elbow on his knee, his chin resting on his palm. "Let me think about that."

Thomas lifted his gaze and found Miss Seaton watching him.

Thank you, she mouthed to him. He considered that she might actually believe her job to be in danger.

They visited three more houses, each family accommodating and cheerful, as Thomas knew they would be.

"Mr. Langley," Miss Seaton said as she joined him by the fire of the Downs's cottage while the children sucked on honey candy. She spoke in a whisper. "I must ask. Did you talk to all of these people before we came?"

He bowed his head to Mr. Downs, who gestured from across the room that the sleigh was nearly ready. "Why do you ask, Miss Seaton?"

"Because they pull off with the sleigh to load their contribution before any of the children ask for it."

"Ah, yes, that." He leaned closer, never appreciating the proximity required when whispering so much as right now in front of this fire with Miss Seaton. "Would it make any difference to you if I told you that I did?"

He watched her from the corner of his eye, a slight pout in her expression as she considered.

"No, I suppose not, as long as the children are unaware. Though I wanted this to be a growing experience. One doesn't truly grow unless one has to struggle. My father would say, 'Paul was only Saul until the road to Damascus.'"

He frowned. "You think I've made it too easy for them."

"No. No, not at all. They are learning. I just wonder what they would do if they came across one not so eager to share."

"Do you not want people to share?" It fascinated him, figuring out her mind.

She smiled, a little shake to her head. "Of course I want them to share. But life isn't always easy, is it, Mr. Langley? Life is not easy on Furrows Street. Nor at the vicarage. Nor away at school."

"Nor at Canterwood?" he asked, more of a challenge than a question.

She shrugged at the fire. "It is a beautiful, ideal place. But ask the hands that keep it beautiful, that manage things from beneath to uphold the ideal, and the answer would be that life is not easy." She met his gaze. "It's unpredictable. It is work. But you would find strength along that road. Deep, fought-for strength."

He could not look away. "You keep surprising me, Miss Seaton."

Her chin lifted a little in that way that warned him to tread softly. "Because I speak my mind?"

He shook his head. "No. Because you speak mine."

His hand, as if it had a mind of its own, lifted toward the curl against her cheek. He paused just in time and pulled away, gripping his hat behind his back once more.

A look of apprehension crossed her face, and she quickly turned back to the fire.

Mr. Downs appeared. "Vicar?"

Thomas turned, suddenly unsure that he should be speaking at all. Drat. The old gentleman was saying something, but Thomas was only aware that Miss Seaton had not turned around, was still staring into the fire, worrying her fingers in the folds of her cloak.

"Yes," he heard himself say. "Thank you, Mr. Downs. God bless you. We'll be on our way now."

He gathered the children, glancing to see Miss Seaton tying the bow of Sophia's bonnet with some concentration.

What had he said? Something about reading his mind? He placed his hat on his head and took a deep, steadying breath. A hand wrapped around his and he looked down.

Helena smiled up at him. "Where are we going next, Mr. Langley?"

"We are heading," he said, gripping her hand as they descended the front steps, "toward Damascus."

"Will they have tea?"

"I certainly hope so, Helena."

CHAPTER 5

JULIA COULDN'T SETTLE IN HER seat and wished she'd joined the girls in the back under their woolen blankets and fur pelt. She half-listened to Alger's questions and Mr. Langley's responses, though the deeper timbre of the vicar's voice seemed to enter her head and circulate through her whole being, as if that particular characteristic of his could be breathed in. What was this that both called to her and unsettled her so? And what was that exchange in front of the fireplace at the Downs? Had he really meant to say that her words were his thoughts? Surely not all the time. That would be dreadful. No, just a few times, apparently. When she'd surprised him with it.

She caught herself smiling and squelched it.

Twisting her gloved hands in the skirt of her cloak, Julia glanced at Mr. Langley. As he spoke, she found the gleam in his eye he hid so well and the movement of his mouth as he huffed out puffs of breath into the cold air. The bloom of his cheeks as he found her watching him.

Oh, heavens. She turned away, aware that he'd paused mid-sentence when he'd found her staring like a basset hound.

The questions ceased as the sleigh turned up a grand, tree-lined lane, the stark branches nearly touching overhead. The road turned to circumnavigate a nearly frozen pond then opened up to a rolling, white lawn.

Julia drew in a breath as she caught site of the house set upon a hill. "How grand," she said. Indeed, "house" was not the right word. This was not like the columned pale-brick estates they'd visited, nor the sturdy, sandy stone boxes of Canterwood. Three stories loomed tall with gables atop the highest windows, flanked on each side by a turret. Parapets crowned the west wing, and still more of the edifice remained hidden from her view in a lofty copse of trees as they approached from the south. It wasn't that she'd never seen a great hall or even a castle, but she'd never seen *this* one, so close to where she'd been living for three months.

Of course, why would a governess ever have an invitation or even an excuse to visit such a residence? "What is this place?" she asked, hearing the awe in her voice.

She tore her gaze away from the approach and looked at Mr. Langley. He pulled in a deep breath and blew it out. "Antony Hall, seat to the late Earl of Antony." He turned to Julia. "My home."

Her mouth opened to reply, but no sound came out.

"Is it a castle?" Sophia asked. The girls had risen from their bench and were turned around, peering between the others.

"No. But I believe it was designed to resemble one. It's no Alnwick. But it was something to explore when I was a boy, certainly." He peered back at Sophia. "If we didn't get caught." He winked and she grinned.

"This . . ." Julia started. She looked at the place again. "This is your home?"

"Was. Though I didn't live in this part of it. My father is steward here. Our cottage is beyond. It's empty while they're away." He gestured to the north. "But the earl's son, the Viscount Lord Antony, had children, and I was a child and well . . ." he looked back at Sophia. "There are no classes among children, are there?"

The girl shook her head as if they'd shared a great secret.

But then his chin dropped, his smile faded, and he turned his attention back to the team of horses and pulling the sleigh up to the front of a grand marble stairway. Indeed, the entire house appeared to be made of golden marble.

But the vicar didn't stop at the front and instead continued around the side to a servant's entry.

"Alger, help your sisters," Mr. Langley said as he jumped down. "Take care, the tramped snow here is slick."

As Alger obeyed, the vicar crossed to Julia's side and held his arms up, an unreadable expression on his face. When she paused, he only waited. Tenuously, she rested her hands on his shoulders, and at her touch, his hands gripped her waist and he lifted her down. When her feet met the ground, her boot slipped on the packed snow, and he caught her, his arm coming around her, pressing her to his shoulder. She found herself gripping his arms.

After a moment, he spoke into her ear. "Are you all right?"

She found herself a little breathless but otherwise unharmed. "Quite."

He lifted as she found her footing, and he gently extricated himself from her fingers, taking her elbow instead. Then he carefully reached and moved an escaped curl stuck to her cheek, all the while his expression stern.

"Thank you," she said. "Did I hurt you?"

He broke into a smile that almost startled her in its brilliance. "No." He shook his head, clearly attempting to reduce his smile to nothing once more. He led her to a door several steps down, set deeply into the stone exterior.

"Why do you fight that so?" she asked, still recovering from her slip and his arm around her.

"Fight what?" He refused to look at her.

She opened her mouth to tell him, when a wiry older woman in a house uniform opened the door and threw a shawl over her head.

"What's this? The best vicar in all of Northumberland is paying us a visit?" she asked.

He smiled again. "Hello, Mrs. Reid."

She smiled back, shaking her head. "And you've come to the side door? You're not ten anymore, Tom." She began shooing them all inside. "You're an upstanding young man with a nice living to offer anyone, including this fine young lady, and you come to my door."

The vicar cast Julia a sideways glance just as her mouth popped open at the woman's presumption. She closed it promptly.

Mrs. Reid only continued. "Oh well. You've never been one to put on airs, have you? Come in out of the cold. It's bread-making day, so we're all a bit toasty. The children look cold and tired. You'll be needing sustenance. How cunning of you to call at tea."

Julia noted the eagerness in the children's eyes at the mention of tea as they entered an alcove set between a servants' gathering room and the kitchen. They'd been given a treat or two but had missed luncheon. Mrs. Reid waved them to the left, and they followed.

"If it's no trouble," Mr. Langley said, removing his hat.

"No trouble 't all. My lord is expecting you," she said, offering a bemused smile. "Though he won't be joining you here in the kitchen."

"At this very minute, Mrs. Reid, I'm considering taking tea in the larder."

Mrs. Reid shook her head, feigning shock. "You'll do no such thing."

Mr. Langley touched Julia's elbow again. "Mrs. Reid, may I introduce to you Miss Julia Seaton?"

Mrs. Reid bobbed a curtsy.

"How do you do, Mrs. Reid?" Julia said. "I'm sorry we surprised you."

"Not at all, dear. The vicar gave word he was coming, though he did not mention the company he was bringing with him. But he also knows we throw our backs into low tea here and there's plenty. You're more than welcome."

Julia smiled, believing her. "Do you come to church, Mrs. Reid? I have not seen you there."

Mr. Langley leaned toward Julia. "That is because Antony Hall *does* have its own chapel and its own vicarage beside it."

"Oh, forgive me," Julia said. "I did not think."

"No matter," he said. He turned back to Mrs. Reid. "And these turnips," he gestured to the children, "are Master Algernon and Misses Sophia and Helena Stanhope of Canterwood. Miss Seaton is their governess. They are on a quest."

Mrs. Reid looked more impressed than she should have been. "Master Richard's neices and nephew? Hello, and what quest might you be up to on a cold day like this? Come, let's unwrap you and set your things by a fire. Cynthia! Come take the outer things and find a spot to warm them. It's a good thing you all didn't come on washing day. Underthings everywhere." The children began to disrobe. "I'll let the master know you're here. Jim? Where's Jim? Henry, go tell Lord Antony that the vicar is here. And tell him and lady that tea is ready." She put her hands on her hips. "You really should have come to the front door, Tom."

"Then I'd never have seen you, and that would have been a travesty."

Mrs. Reid, blushed and grinned. "Oh. How I miss you little'uns running 'round." She turned to Alger. "Do you know I've known the vicar since he was five years old? Just a baby."

Helena spoke up. "I'm five!"

"Just as I suspected. Well, now that you're all uncloaked, let's get you set down and tucked in. We've cold lamb sandwiches with mustard, figs, cheese, and an apple cake with cream that melts in your mouth." She turned to Julia. "I assume the children will be eating here in the kitchen, or will they be joining you in the sitting room?" Mrs. Reid arched a brow. "The nursery is a bit of a relic at the moment, but I suppose we could send someone to sweep it out."

"Oh." Julia looked to Mr. Langley. "I should think the children would be more comfortable here." Helena was already seating herself on a chair at a long table and making conversation with a girl peeling potatoes. "Mr. Langley?"

"Certainly. Let's get everyone fed, and then we'll have the children make their plea."

"Oof, so your quest includes Lord Antony?" Mrs. Reid pursed her lips. "In that case, you all should get food in your stomachs first. Including him who will decide your fate. Let's get you upstairs as proper. Miss, would you care to freshen up?"

Julia sighed, grateful. "Yes, please."

❧

Tea was a stoic affair. The Viscount Edmund Antony III and his wife greeted Julia and Mr. Langley with all the formality of royalty, though Julia sensed an underlying displeasure at their visit. She wondered at that. Mr. Langley was not only their steward's son and one who grew up here with their own children, but also a vicar. And a kind one, too.

"We are grandparents now, Mr. Langley," Lady Antony was saying as she picked up a fig.

"Wonderful," he said, pausing from his cup. "And . . . how is Abigayle?"

Julia noted the hesitation in his asking.

"The marchioness is doing quite well, thank you. They're in Hertfordshire of course. They are the delight of the *ton* again, now that her confinement is over. A baby boy. They couldn't be happier."

Julia watched this exchange with interest. A muscle twitched in the vicar's cheek. But his countenance softened.

"What a blessing," he said. "I'm truly happy for her. For them all."

Lady Antony paused in lifting her fork. She met his gaze, and something changed there. Julia would have guessed she saw a bit of longing. "Thank you, Tom," she said softly.

He nodded, and they resumed eating.

The viscount cleared his throat. "Has Mr. Langley told you, Miss Seaton, how he and my son would climb trees?"

"Edmund, I don't think—" Lady Antony said.

"The two of them and the Stanhope boy. They would dare each other to climb higher and higher every time."

Mr. Langley wiped his mouth with his napkin and set it down. "We were boys."

"Yes. Boys forget who they are in the world. Some think they can climb, when they've no business reaching for the first branch."

"Edmund, don't."

"Hush, Luisa."

Julia felt her cheeks burn with distress for everyone in this massive, ornate house.

Thomas stood, his demeanor calm. "We were innocent children. I think I misjudged my welcome. I am sorry for this imposition. I thank you again, most graciously, my lord, for the living you have bestowed upon me. It is everything I wish, next to the return of our boys, our friends, back from the war. We grew up, didn't we? Ted embraced his position in society and in life. And though I am no longer a thought of his, I will always think of him fondly. As I do this place." He looked around, and his gaze landed on Julia. "Shall we ask the children in now?"

She blinked. Then nodded and rose. The viscount stood. "Excuse me, Lord Antony, Lady Antony," she said. "The children are here with a purpose. Concerning Christmas. I'll return shortly."

"This is highly out of the ordinary," Lord Antony said gruffly.

She looked again at Mr. Langley as the viscount and his wife had a small exchange. To her surprise, he smiled warmly, and the tightening in her chest that had grown during the recent conversation loosened. As she hurried past him, her hand brushed his, and in that instant, he wrapped his fingers around hers, and squeezed them gently.

She looked up at him, her eyes searching.

"This is their Damascus," he said quietly.

She thought she understood and continued on to the children, the warmth of the vicar's hand lingering, chasing away the discomfort of that miserable conversation. How had he done that—stood and squelched whatever point the viscount had meant to make? No wonder smiles did not come so readily to Mr. Langley. He was not dismal. In a way—in his own wonderful way—he was the opposite.

The children needed a little cleanup before their entry into the dining hall. But when they were ready, Julia ushered them in, the girls first, holding hands, and then Alger behind. As they approached the viscount, even Helena held back. Mr. Langley joined Julia, and she was surprised at the relief she found just from his being nearer. He introduced the children as he had before, and the girls gave little curtsies. Alger managed a fairly impressive bow.

"Is the rest of your house this beautiful?" Helena asked Lady Antony, wide-eyed.

The woman smiled. "I think it is."

Helena smiled back, satisfied.

"My lord?" Alger began, only a touch shaky. "We are collecting firewood and coal for those who might not have enough to be warm on Christmas."

Lord Antony frowned and glanced at Mr. Langley, who kept his focus on the children.

"Why might they not have enough?" the man asked.

"Because, my lord, they are poor," Alger said.

"Why are they poor?"

Alger hesitated.

"Because," Helena said bravely, "some of their papas are gone. They're at the war, helping to stop Mr. Napoleon. It's taking a very long time."

"And my lord?" said Sophia, stepping forward a little. "Some of them have many children, or they are sick and have to spend their money on medicine. They must choose whether to be cold or be sick."

The viscount lowered his head toward her. "How do you know this?"

"My mama takes me to visit them. We bring them soup and bread. But Mama isn't here right now. She might not be home for Christmas." Here,

Sophia's chin quivered. "So, we're here, and we're doing what Mama would do. We're trying to help."

The viscount's frown deepened, and he straightened, looking at Mr. Langley. "What is this?" he asked, as if the children hadn't spoken at all. Indeed, they looked at one another with confusion on their faces.

"Charity, sir. Have you not heard of it? Corinthians, chapter thirteen. Paul." The vicar smiled at Julia. "'And now abideth faith, hope, charity, these three.'" He turned back to Lord Antony. "'But the greatest of these is charity.'"

"That's the Bible," Helena offered.

Lord Antony peered down at her. "I know it's the Bible." He glared at Julia then Mr. Langley. "I did not give you this living so you could show up at my house to preach at me. And I certainly didn't give you a living so you could rob me to give to those who won't help themselves. I'm done here, Luisa. Show our guests out."

Helena drew in a stuttered breath as tears spilled down her cheeks. "We didn't mean to upset you, my lord."

The viscount paused. "Of course you didn't. Excuse me." He left the room briskly.

Julia rushed to Helena's aid with a handkerchief as Sophia wrapped her arm around her sister. "I am so proud of all of you," she said, though it seemed of little comfort. "You tried your best, and you can leave here knowing that."

Lady Antony spoke quietly behind her. "Forgive my husband. He received bad news just before your arrival. A friend, a naval captain, has been gravely wounded. The war affects even a viscount, I'm afraid. Still," she paused and then decided not to finish.

"I'm sorry to hear that. I should not have presumed to call as I did," Mr. Langley said.

"No. No, Tom, you of all people should be able to visit us when you can. I'm afraid it wouldn't have made a difference either way." She gave him a weak smile then sobered. "I must apologize to you. I've been petty." She put a handkerchief to her nose.

"Come now," Mr. Langley said. "It's Christmas. Let us be above things that happened so long ago."

"Thank you, Tom. I'll tell your mother what a good man you've become."

"She may not believe you," he said with that subtle hint of mischief Julia was coming to know.

Lady Antony shook her head, but her eyes were a bit brighter.

The warm kitchen was a welcome relief, and Mrs. Reid helped them get the children bundled up in hearth-warm coats and muffs. While Mrs. Reid's chatter cheered the children, Mr. Langley helped Julia with her cloak. She turned to him, and a look passed between them—one of resolve. But when her fingers refused to do what they should, he had to help her with the toggle at her neck.

"Are you upset with me?" he asked, his brow furrowed.

He wasn't the only one frowning. "I asked for tribulation," she said. "How can I be upset with you?"

"I hoped it would be different."

"I believe you did. I also believe, after my brief time here, that different would have been miraculous."

The corner of his mouth drew up, and he studied her face.

"What?" she asked. Honestly, would his smile bring hers out every time? Sure enough, there it was.

"It is the season of miracles," he said.

She nodded, and his expression deepened. He hadn't let go of her cloak.

"It's warm in here," she said, scarcely breathing.

"Baking day," he said quietly.

Julia felt as though baking day and the kitchen were suddenly far off, as if a cloak of another kind had wrapped itself around only her and the vicar, and it wasn't solemn or awkward or silent.

It was lovely.

"Well, vicar, the children are bundled, and your team's been pulled around."

Mr. Langley drew away from Julia, leaving her pulling in a soft breath.

"We'll be off, then," he said. "It was a delight seeing you again, Mrs. Reid. Thank you for your help with the children."

"You're welcome to visit anytime. We're proud of you. All of us, though it might be harder for some to show it." Of course, Mrs. Reid would have already heard about the goings on in the sitting room. She lowered her voice and leaned toward the vicar. "And don't be shy bringing this one 'round, neither. I've a feeling she won't be a governess very much longer."

"Oh." Julia flustered at tying on her bonnet. "I assure you, I—" She finished the bow and straightened. "I like my job."

Mr. Langley shook his head at Mrs. Reid. "You are wicked, Mrs. Reid." He lowered his hat over his brow and turned to usher the children out the door.

"Is that the vicar speaking," the woman asked after him, "or the boy I know as well as my own?"

He ignored her.

Mrs. Reid shook her head at Julia. "Never you mind, miss. I didn't say a word." She hushed her voice conspiratorially. "But I will say this: That one there," she nodded to Mr. Langley's back. "A heart of gold and loyal to the end. Think on that, miss."

"I am not a spaniel, Mrs. Reid," Mr. Langley said, his back still turned.

Mrs. Reid only rolled her eyes.

It was all Julia could do to get herself out the door past the waiting vicar and take his proffered hand to help her up onto the bench. She was sure her cheeks must have been roses. She began to wonder if this project of theirs was worth the stirring of so many feelings. She wasn't used to keeping up with such a variety in so short a time. As Mr. Langley climbed on, she looked around.

"Where's Alger?"

"He's in back, restoring his sisters with his ideas for the Christmas play."

She looked behind them and sure enough, Alger sat with his arms around both his sisters, their heads together in conspiracy. They were good children.

She faced forward again, keenly aware of the space on the bench between her and Mr. Langley.

"I hope," he said, giving the reins a snap so the sleigh lurched forward, "you don't give Mrs. Reid's predictions too much weight. She likes to tease."

"Oh. Of course. I mean, of course not. I don't. I mean, I won't." Dear, what had happened to her vocabulary? "Why would I?" She felt suddenly hollow.

He continued, his hat pulled low. "I'm not looking to—I mean, I'm not looking for—"

"Oh! Neither am I. I mean, I need to work. Of course I do." She shook her head and swallowed nervously. "What with Mother having to leave the vicarage . . ." She pulled up the lap blanket, twisting it in her hands. "I was to marry a friend of my mother's family, you see. That was the plan. But it turned out he liked the daughter of a sugar baron more than me . . . Who can blame him, really? My father's patron let us the only place we could afford. So I need to work, or . . ." Oh no, tears couldn't possibly be starting now. Why was she blathering so? "I'm sounding like a charity endeavor myself now, aren't I? How appropriate."

She couldn't look at him, but his gloved hand covered hers, stilling it.

"Compassion and pity are two different things, Miss Seaton."

His quiet words helped.

She gave her head another shake, determined to change the subject, and looked up at the tremendous hall as they passed.

"Did you love her?" she asked, immediately regretting the question.

"Who?" he asked.

She couldn't very well now pretend she hadn't asked. She winced and watched the snow. "The marchioness."

Several moments passed before he answered. She held her breath as he shifted on the bench. "I suppose I did. Years ago. In the way that young people do when they grow up together and then discover that . . . well, that they were growing up." He shook his head. "We were very young. Lord Antony discovered our admiration for one another, and within days I was sent to continue my schooling at Eton. I never saw Abigayle again." He faced her. "She was my friend, first and foremost, Miss Seaton. And that is what hurt the most. A few years later, Ted found our circles very different, and he too faded from my life."

She saw the pain etched in his expression. "I'm so sorry," she said.

He shook his head and faced forward again. "I guess that's why Canterwood holds such a dear place in my heart. I was an equal there." He smiled. "It became a second home."

"I am glad of that, Mr. Langley. It is good to have a place where one belongs."

She took a deep breath and turned her thinking to the children. That always cleared her dizzying thoughts. "It was worth a try, coming to this house today, wasn't it? For the charity. Say it was worth a try."

"It was worth a try, Miss Seaton." His expression grew most sincere. "Most endeavors of real value are."

She nodded.

"Mr. Langley! Vicar!"

They both turned behind them. A man she assumed to be Jim ran to them with three others following, all of them laden with large bundles. Mr. Langley pulled the sleigh to a stop.

"These," Jim said, catching his breath, "are for the charity. Three sacks of coal." The men threw the burlap sacks onto the sleigh bed amidst triumphant sounds from the children.

He came around on the vicar's side.

"Are these from Lady Antony, then?" Mr. Langley asked. "Do give her our sincerest thanks."

Jim shook his head. "Lord Antony gave me the order himself, sir. Merry Christmas."

Mr. Langley and Julia sat stunned.

"And this one," said a lighter voice on Julia's side, "is from Mrs. Reid. A ham, apples, walnuts, cheese, and this morning's bread. For your charity luncheon. 'We won't be missing it none,' she says!" The girl, Cynthia, heaved the bag right toward Julia on the bench so that with a yelp, Julia found herself just next to Mr. Langley.

"Happy Christmas," the girl said and waved as she walked away.

"Happy Christmas," Julia said, holding her bonnet to her head and feeling quite bewildered.

She looked at the vicar, who looked back, just as bewildered and very close.

"The season of miracles," he whispered.

Julia swallowed. "Indeed."

After another moment, he snapped the reins, and they moved forward once more, Julia's shoulder brushing against his with every jostle and dip.

She glanced again at the sack of food that could have easily gone in the back with the rest. "I believe Mrs. Reid to be a very shrewd woman," Julia said.

He grinned beneath his hat. "Indeed."

⁓ℓ⁓

At the end of a very long day spent mostly by the side of a clever, pretty, and refreshingly honest governess, his fingers still sticky from helping paste seashells onto a glove box, Thomas Langley returned to the silent vicarage in real danger of forgetting why he'd been so dead set against marrying at the age of twenty-four. And of wondering obsessively why on earth anyone would give up Julia Seaton for a sugar baron's daughter.

He certainly wouldn't.

It was that thought that kept him up later than he needed.

CHAPTER 6

THE HOUSEHOLD WAS IN AN uproar.

Evergreen boughs graced the window boxes and banisters, and a large wreath hung above the front entry. Sophia and Helena had completed their homemade gifts. The Christmas Eve luncheon had been a success, and Julia couldn't say who came away merrier—those who received the gift of warmth this Christmas or the Stanhope children. When Mr. Langley had returned them to Canterwood in his own modest carriage afterward, the children's joy had been added to in finding their parents just stepping down from their hired stage. Julia was sure she had not seen a happier reunion. And a quieter joy, but a joy nonetheless: Lady Teresa had received a letter from her son Richard, who was healthy and spoke of coming home.

Even now, Julia smiled while the chaos continued behind her. At this moment, she stood at the window of the nursery, the lace curtains pulled back, watching the snow fall, thinking of that sleigh ride. And the snow. And wondering that she had not felt alone at all these past few days.

"Ahem."

She turned to find Mr. Langley looking quite perplexed, his hands clasped behind his back. Her hand came to her mouth, and she could not stop the giggle that arose behind it.

"It's a bit drastic, isn't it?" he asked, quietly enough for the children not to hear.

Someone, likely Alger, had wrapped an aubergine silk scarf abundantly around his head and fastened it with a brooch, and instead of a waistcoat, Mr. Langley wore his white shirt, and another silk scarf knotted over his breeches at his hip; this one she recognized as one of Lady Teresa's fringed shawls in a lovely emerald green. His riding boots finished it off, or so she thought.

She peered closer at this man who had been by her side almost constantly the past three days. "You have—"

Before she could finish, he reached up to his ear, pulled off a single earring, and held it out to her. "A man has boundaries that will not be crossed," he said, his cheeks coloring.

She took the earring and pocketed it. "Most certainly," she said as she eyed the fringed scarf. "Innkeepers most likely would hide their baubles in a box with a lock during tax season, anyhow."

He nodded seriously then paused as he caught the delight she was having in teasing him.

She grinned. Alger had his pirate after all. "You look like a fine keeper of a prosperous and crowded inn."

He ran his hand over his face and sighed.

"You will still be vicar and regarded as such when all this is over," she said. "And you will have won the adoration of three of your parishioners for all of their days."

"Not four of my parishioners?" he asked, his brow arched.

"Well," she said, "we shall see how it all turns out. Remember, you are in this for forgiveness."

"Hmm." He glanced down at his costume. "I believe this is more than I bargained for."

She smiled and continued to do so until he broke and smiled back. He looked her over.

"Where is your costume?" he asked.

"I've been helping Tilde and poor Nelson. I don't know how the children got him and James to agree to take part in this. I take that back—yes, I do. They give those looks with the round eyes and say the clever words."

"The little imps," he murmured.

"Vicar, I'm astonished."

He smiled. "Are you?"

He held her gaze. His nearness the past few days had made her brave, and she'd determined that looking him in the eyes could quite possibly become habit-forming if she wasn't careful. He watched her, expectant.

"I suppose it takes one to know one," she said.

He laughed out loud. It was a glorious sound.

"Miss Seaton?" She felt a tug on her skirt.

Julia looked down to find Sophia waiting at her hip wearing a white gown and a feathered circlet atop her head. "Yes, dearest?"

"It's your turn. Tilde and Nessa are all turned out, and you are the last."

"All right, then." She held out her hand for Sophia to take her away, noting a definite uptake in her own pulse, as she suddenly grew nervous.

"Miss Seaton."

She turned back to Mr. Langley. "Yes?"

"I have something for you." From behind his back, he produced a pinecone. A single, fat pinecone.

She looked from it to him.

"For luck," he said.

Slowly, she reached for it, the texture both rough and smooth against her fingertips, the heft of its weight on her palm as she closed her hand around it. Happy memories of devotion flooded her.

Sophia tugged on her other arm.

She looked up at him. "Thank you," she managed to say.

He bowed. "I only regret being unable to locate your bonnet."

She smiled and then allowed Sophia to lead her away. That did not stop her from looking back over her shoulder, where Mr. Langley stood watching her go.

～∾

Candles and lanterns lit the drawing room, and the hum and crackle from the grand fireplace soon became the prominent sound as they readied to begin. Thomas waited behind one of the wood-paneled screens that had been brought into the drawing room and placed on either side of a simple but sturdy framed stable; a manger of hay stood at its center. Little Helena and James, Canterwood's stable master and an impressive sport about all of this, waited with him. Across from him behind the other screen, Miss Seaton waited with the other players. She peered at him around Tilde and gave him a nervous smile. He nodded in return, feeling a mote of assurance, along with that exasperating uptick of his pulse that came whenever Miss Seaton entered his vision.

Alger stood in the center of the "stage" in his fur cape and beech wood staff, striking in his fearlessness. And what was there to fear? Frank and Ophelia had returned as promised. The expressions on theirs and Lady Teresa's face were of anticipated delight. And the boy had faced Lord Antony himself and come out winning.

This just might work, he thought to himself, and offered up a silent prayer anyway.

"Ladies and gentlemen," Alger began. "I am John the Baptist. I came before my cousin to prepare the way for Him who would be King of Kings, and I don't mind that job one bit."

Thomas grinned.

"And so tonight, it is my duty and honor to tell you the story of how the Savior of the world was born. Behold, there went out a decree from Caesar Augustus that all the world should be taxed."

Nelson, in all his gravity, was gently prodded out from behind the opposite screen, draped in a white sheet and wearing a circlet of crisp ivy vine.

"I decree that all the world shall be taxed," he said then turned and disappeared behind the screen.

Miss Seaton beamed with delight.

Thomas quickly drew his gaze away from her and looked to James, but the man already had Helena upon old Chaser, the wheeled toy horse from the Stanhope nursery.

John the Baptist did his job, announcing the couple's journey to Bethlehem, and little Mary sat wistfully upon Chaser as James—Joseph—pulled her across the staged area and then back again.

With a jolt, Thomas backed away from his place behind the panels, realizing his part came next.

"And so it was, the day came that she should be delivered. But there was no room for them at the inn."

James knocked at the panel frame, and the thing wobbled, but Thomas, determined to do well by both the children and the subject, kept the thing from falling over and stepped around. A gasp, a cough, and a snicker from the audience did not ease his discomfort.

"Please, sir," James began a bit woodenly. Brilliant with live horses, the man was clearly out of his element. "My wife is nearly delivered. Do you have room for us in your inn?"

Thomas looked between James and Helena and shook his head. "My inn is full of taxpayers . . . and . . ." he glanced to where Alger watched him eagerly, "and ruffians," he said.

"Goodness," murmured Lady Teresa, and Thomas covered a smile. Alger beamed.

He continued, his only lines not even scripture, and yet he hesitated to say these next words for the distress they would have caused on that night so long ago. "Forgive me. I have no room for you here."

James turned, convincingly dejected. Helena sighed heavily, and then she straightened her little self on that wooden horse and turned to her audience. "Do not fret. I am determined that we shall find a miracle."

Her words, in her small yet steady voice, moved him.

"Wait." Thomas held up a hand as Alger had instructed him. "Perhaps I do have a place for the lady. Follow me."

He led Joseph and Mary to the makeshift stable.

"This is much better than the noisy inn," said Helena. "It's quiet and warm. Thank you, kind sir."

Thomas bowed low. "Good night, my lady." Then he and James pulled a screen of Chinese silk from the conservatory in front of the stable, and Thomas returned to his place behind the wooden panels and pulled off his ghastly headpiece and sash, trading them for a straw gardener's hat and a shepherd's staff.

"And there were in the same country shepherds abiding in their field, keeping watch over their flock by night," John the Baptist said. "But their housekeeper wouldn't allow actual sheep in this particular field, so they watched over Fitz the Bunny and Mr. Bingle."

Thomas grabbed the velvet rabbit as the audience laughed, and emerged from his hiding place, meeting Miss Seaton, who was holding the children's stuffed bear. She wore a muslin headdress tied with a green ribbon around her forehead, and her hair was down, falling long and soft around her shoulders. She set the bear down on the floor, and as she rose, she looked up at him.

The lift of her chin and the dance of firelight in her eyes made him pause. After a moment, she took Fitz the Bunny from his arms and set it down and looked at the ceiling with a blush in her cheeks. He blinked and followed her gaze.

"The stars are quite bright tonight. Look at that one," she said as she pointed.

"Unusually bright," he said, glancing at her once again. "And beautiful."

She flickered a glance his way, and he tried to stick to the script. "I wonder if it means something," he said.

"And, lo," Alger—John continued. "The angel of the Lord came upon them, and the glory of the Lord shown round about them. And they were sore afraid."

Sophia emerged all in white with the largest lantern she could lift. She held it aloft as Thomas and Miss Seaton fell to their knees and feigned fear. The entire room waited for her line. And waited.

The child seemed frozen.

Next to him he heard Miss Seaton barely whisper, "Fear not—"

"Fear not!" Sophia exclaimed, and Thomas jumped. Miss Seaton graciously contained her amusement.

Sophia swallowed and gathered herself. "Fear not," she said more gently. "For I bring you good tidings of great joy, which shall be to all people. For unto you is born this day in the city of David, a Savior, which is Christ the Lord.

And you shall find the babe wrapped in swaddling clothes, lying in a manger." Sophia's relief manifested in a brilliant smile at Miss Seaton, then at her parents.

She set the lantern down in front of her as two young housemaids joined her in white dresses and feather halos, and the three of them sang, "Whilst Shepherds Watched Their Flocks by Night," their unrefined voices combining rather sweetly.

The angels then backed away, taking their lantern with them, and the room grew hushed. Thomas stood in the darkened lighting and held his hand to Julia, assisting her up. The pleasant shock of her warm skin against his made him wonder why gloves had ever been brought into daily fashion.

Miss Seaton smiled at him. "Let us go," she said, and heaven help him, he believed she was truly eager to visit a newborn babe in the far-off city of Bethlehem.

On impulse, he bowed low over her soft hand, resisting the urge to press it with a kiss. He rose and with all earnestness said, "We'll go now."

They gathered their "sheep" and together walked behind the screen. He removed his shepherd's hat, and they each found a space in the panel to peer through. Thomas's heart pounded in his chest, but it wasn't from the playacting, nor from the spirit that had pervaded Canterwood's drawing room this evening.

No, it was the nearness of Miss Seaton. Her goodness and hope for those around her. Her determination and ability to see potential reached for. It was the stripe of candlelight shining from her brow to her neck and the lovely way her hair fell, gently curling as she watched the play her young charge had made as a gift to his parents. It was as Miss Seaton had said. Alger had interpreted a good thing and was applying it to his life in the nursery, a life he would soon leave for a larger world. But this experience would not leave him. Thomas wished for the boy to keep it ever in his heart. Just as he himself would.

John the Baptist and a now formally attired Nelson had drawn the Chinese screen away, having revealed Joseph, Mary, and the baby Jesus—a doll of Helena's she'd introduced to him as Lucy-Anne—in her arms.

"What a beautiful little scene," Miss Seaton whispered.

"You were perfectly right, Miss Seaton," he answered softly. "About the play."

He turned to find her watching him, lips slightly parted. She closed them and nodded.

Alger—John—took his place again as narrator and drew their attention once more. "And Mary brought forth her newborn son and wrapped Him in swaddling clothes and laid Him in a manger."

Both Thomas and Miss Seaton stood at the same time. "There's our cue," she said, just as he said, "Here we go." But they had stood facing one another, much closer than he'd expected, and neither of them moved.

"Miss Seaton," he whispered, just as she opened her mouth to speak.

She paused and looked away, a small smile at her lips.

He hadn't meant to say her name like that, nor had he meant to take her hand again. But he had. Her gaze drew back to his.

He swallowed. "Forgive me once more, Miss Seaton."

"For what?" she whispered back.

"I believe," he said, keeping his voice low enough for only her to hear, "that I have grown fond of this."

Her brow rose. "Playacting?"

He shook his head.

"Shepherding, then."

"No," he said.

"Hiding behind screens?"

He smiled at her provocations. "Possibly."

After another moment passed, she lowered her lashes. "What is it you've grown fond of, Mr. Langley?"

He braced himself, feeling his time would very soon be up, and this opportunity to speak might pass into the oblivion of his former convictions. "I've grown very fond," he said, "of being near you."

Her gaze lifted, her eyes round. "Oh, heavens," she very faintly replied.

Thomas furrowed his brow, uncertain of her response.

A loud crack followed by a cry from Helena sounded from the stable. This was not in the script. Miss Seaton turned and rushed around the panel, Thomas on her heels.

But Frank and Ophelia were faster. In all her fineness, Ophelia knelt where the little girl had dropped to the floor in sobs, and wrapped her in her arms.

Miss Seaton stopped. "What has happened? Is Helena hurt?"

Ophelia shook her head. Helena looked up, eyes red and rimmed with tears. "I broke baby Jesus," she wailed. She held up Lucy-Anne, and one arm dangled loosely in its sleeve, no longer attached at the elbow.

"Oh, dear," Lady Teresa said at Thomas's right. "This is problematic."

"She was trying to wrap it in swaddling clothes and it dropped," Ophelia said.

Miss Seaton crouched down in front of Helena, who peeked at her from her mother's embrace. "May I?" she asked.

Helena nodded, and Miss Seaton carefully took Lucy-Anne from the child's arms.

Thomas watched her caress the doll's hair and face, then tenderly remove the broken arm from the doll's sleeve. After assessing the damage, Miss Seaton looked up.

"Tilde, will you fetch me a long strip of muslin for bandaging?"

Tilde bobbed. "Yes, miss."

The servants must have moved quickly. The girl returned in moments.

With bandage in hand, and under Helena's attentive eye, Miss Seaton wrapped the doll's arm from shoulder to wrist and back again, tucking in the end. She gently re-dressed Lucy-Anne and straightened the gown. Then she picked up the fallen swaddling and handed them both out to Helena.

"I think baby Jesus would love to be swaddled now, after this little mishap. Little ones need love when things take a bad turn, don't you agree?"

Helena lifted her head and looked at the doll then back to her mother. She turned to Miss Seaton and nodded.

With Ophelia's help, Helena swaddled the baby. When it was bundled, Ophelia lifted her daughter to standing. "Everything has been so lovely this evening," she said. "Shall we continue?"

Helena cradled the doll and breathed deeply. "I'm ready to be Mary again."

Thomas smiled, and Lady Teresa dabbed at her eyes.

Helena was returned to her place within the stable with Joseph and old Chaser, and the audience returned to their seats. The angels gathered behind the empty manger, while Mary held her baby close to her heart. And Thomas the shepherd, having declared his feelings to Miss Seaton and received an indiscernible reply, stood there, unsure of what to do.

⁓⁓⁓

Julia retrieved Mr. Langley's hat from behind the screen. She paused, reliving the moments before Helena's upset. Her heartbeat sputtered at the memory of his words and his hand so tenderly holding hers.

As she returned to the stage, she found Mr. Langley standing where she'd last seen him, looking lost. As she neared, his gaze focused elsewhere. Most obviously on the floor.

She put the gardener's hat under his nose. He took it, and as he placed it on his head, she held out her hand to him and waited.

Hesitantly he asked, "Shall I take you to Bethlehem, lady shepherd?"

She nodded. "Yes, please, master shepherd. It is my fondest wish to share the angel's tidings to the world. With you."

His gaze lifted to reach hers, and that wobbly feeling she'd felt behind the screen returned. He took her hand, studying it, and drew it around his arm. "Then to Bethlehem we go."

How was it that his simple compliance could fill her with so much delight that her smile could not appear fast enough? Even more delightful was that Thomas returned it.

He faced the audience with Julia on his arm. "We shall glorify and praise God for all the things we have heard and seen."

"And I, John the Baptist," Alger declared, his hand raised in emphasis, "testify that the child grew and waxed strong in spirit, filled with wisdom. And the grace of God was upon Him. For He became my best friend and, indeed, became the best kind of friend to all the world." With his deep bow, the others followed, and the audience stood and clapped their hands.

They were done. They did it. Each and every one of these people surrounding Julia filled her with gratitude.

As Mr. and Mrs. Stanhope and Lady Teresa took turns embracing the children, dabbing their eyes, and declaring it to be the best Christmas they could recall, Julia felt a pull on her arm as Mr. Langley led her aside to the fireplace crackling low.

"Miss Seaton?" he asked, his brown eyes warming her with his gaze. He'd grown serious again.

"Yes, Mr. Langley?"

"Am I forgiven?"

A slow smile came to her face. "Most certainly, Mr. Langley."

He brought her hand to his chest, and she could feel his heart beat beneath his shepherd's shirt. "Miss Seaton?" he asked again.

"Yes, Mr. Langley?"

"May I . . ." He paused and looked as if he were searching for words.

She searched his gaze. "May you . . . ?"

He took a breath and appeared more determined. "May I call on you?"

Her lips parted, and her mind scrambled. To have him call. Just for her. To be near her. "But my work—living here—my family—"

He pulled her closer, his deep gaze diffusing her worries. "We'll sort it out," he said. "All of it."

And that lovely cloak returned, wrapping around only the two of them. "Yes, Mr. Langley. I should like very much for you to call on me."

He breathed a sound of relief. "I feel as if I've reached the top of the highest tree."

She wondered at this man she'd so misjudged. "Wobbly?" she asked.

He smiled with a nod. "Yes. That's it."

He drew Julia's hand up and touched his lips to her skin, his gaze never leaving hers.

"Merry Christmas, Julia," he said.

She could scarce hold herself together. "Merry Christmas . . . Thomas."

A startling applause broke out, and the two of them turned to find the family and a few of the staff watching, clapping their hands, and grinning from ear to ear.

As Julia's face warmed, Mr. Stanhope spoke above the din. "You wouldn't have had anything to do with this, would you, Mother?"

They looked to Lady Teresa, but she merely lifted a brow. "I'm excessively pleased that you think I have that much power." Then she looked at Julia and gave her a wink.

ABOUT THE AUTHOR

NEARLY EVERY ONE OF KRISTA Lynne Jensen's elementary school teachers noted on her report card that she was a "daydreamer." It was not a compliment. So, when Krista grew up, she put those daydreams down on paper for others to enjoy. When she's not writing, she enjoys reading, hiking, her family, and sunshine. But not laundry. She never daydreams about laundry.

Krista writes inspirational romance and fantasy. She is the author of *Of Grace and Chocolate* (2012 Whitney Award Finalist), *The Orchard* (2013 Whiney Award Finalist), *Falling for You* (2014), and *Kisses in the Rain* (2015 Whitney Award Finalist) with Covenant Communications. She has novellas in *Love Unexpected: With All My Heart* and *A Timeless Romance Anthology: Love Letters* (2014). Krista is a member of LDStorymakers and American Night Writers Association (ANWA). Visit her blog at kristalynnejensen.blogspot.com.

Winter Angel

BY ANITA STANSFIELD

For my brother Nathan, an angel in every season.

CHAPTER 1
Daily Bread

London, 1814

MARIAH PRITCHARD PLACED HER GRAY wool scarf strategically over her dark hair so that it hung over her ears to protect them from the cold. She wrapped the ends of the scarf around her neck and left the long ends to hang down so that they were tucked beneath her coat when she put it on and buttoned it. She then pulled on her gloves and picked up the large basket she used for her daily rounds through the streets. The basket was filled to the brim with small rounds of bread—according to Mariah's father they were just the right size to fill a person's empty stomach. Matthew Pritchard had been making his living as a baker since he'd inherited the business from his own father long before Mariah had been born. Her grandparents had all passed on before her birth, but she had been blessed to enjoy the fruits of her paternal grandfather's labors through the bakery he'd left behind.

As Mariah understood it, her father's parents had begun the tradition of taking a basket of bread out into the streets every morning to share it with those who were most in need. Her own parents had carried the tradition forward tirelessly, never missing a day in all the years since, and now Mariah had the privilege of daily sharing the bounty they'd been blessed with by giving a small offering to the cold and hungry who were huddled in doorways and alleys trying to stay warm because they had nowhere to go. Mariah had learned long ago to separate herself emotionally from their suffering. If she thought too hard about the circumstances that might have put people into such situations, and the lack of hope they surely felt each day, she would have gone home each day and locked herself away, consumed by tears. But her father had taught her to simply give the offering of bread to outstretched hands, with a smile and a kind word, and to know that she could not change the lives of these people.

She could not eliminate the suffering of the world, but she could alleviate the hunger of those she came into contact with, and she could find joy and gratitude in being able to do so.

Mariah's offerings of bread to the poor and struggling souls she found on her morning walk were often accepted with a heartfelt "Thank you" or a kind utterance of "God bless you." Mariah graciously accepted their gratitude and pushed away her desire to be able to do more. But she always spent her little excursion in silent prayer on behalf of those she encountered and all whom she didn't who were suffering in poverty and hunger. She reminded herself—as her father often did—that they were doing their small part in a big world to try and alleviate that suffering just a little.

A light skiff of snow had fallen in the night, and Mariah stomped it off her feet before she stepped into the back door of the bakery, her basket now empty but her heart full. She took off her outdoor clothing and hung it on hooks near the door before she donned a clean apron and went through the large kitchen where the baking took place. The warmth of the kitchen was always welcome and soothing after being out in the cold, and she shook off the hovering memory of the people she'd encountered in the streets who were out there trying to stay warm. Instead she focused on the combination of pleasant aromas that were so familiar to her. Matthew Pritchard was well known in this area of London for his refined skills in baking a variety of goods—from the most basic breads and buns to heavenly delicate pastries, many of which were inspired by the French.

Mariah picked up a tray of iced buns her father had been finishing up when she'd left a short while earlier. She took the tray through the doorway that joined the kitchen to the front portion of the bakery where customers came to purchase a variety of baked goods that were lined up on a lovely multi-tiered counter her grandfather had built when he'd first opened the bakery. She set down the tray and exchanged a warm smile with her father, which distracted him for only a moment from taking payment from one of their regular customers for the items she had put into the basket she'd brought with her. Matthew Pritchard was a nice-looking man for his age; he was average height, lean, and even though his hair had turned gray, it hadn't thinned a bit. But most impressionable was his almost continuous smile. Mariah knew he wasn't simply being polite to customers because it was necessary; he found sincere enjoyment in conducting his business, and his smile was practically a permanent fixture on his face. Mariah and her brother both knew that if their father scowled he was truly concerned or upset, because it didn't happen very often.

Mariah walked around the counter of baked goods to the front part of the room, which was decorated with a touch of finery. Blue curtains dotted with little flowers hung at the windows, and contrasting tablecloths rested over the two little tables where customers could sit to enjoy tea with their pastries or buns. The tables were next to large windows on either side of the door, over which a little bell hung that tinkled every time the door opened.

Mariah's younger brother, Mattie—named Matthew after their father, but shortened in order to not confuse the two—was cleaning off one of the tables where two people had just had tea and biscuits, according to the empty teacups and crumbs being cleared away. She assisted Mattie while she teased him and made him smile. She considered him more mature at eleven years old than many adult men she'd encountered in her life; he was polite, kind, and hardworking. Perhaps if she could find a man who was an adult version of Mattie, she might consider giving in to her father's regular nudges toward getting her married. She was twice as old as Mattie and had never met a man who had held her interest for longer than a cup of tea or a shared meal. She'd decided long ago that she'd far prefer to remain a spinster and work here with her father and brother—perhaps one day taking over the bakery in partnership with her brother. She could live a happy and fulfilled life right here; she was certain of it. Her mother had died giving birth to Mattie, and Mariah had observed how her father had grieved over her loss, but with time he had become content with being alone in that regard. She could surely do the same. They were happy here, and she saw no reason to change anything.

The bakery became a bustle of noise and chaos as it always did in the mornings when the majority of their customers came in to purchase baked goods for their household needs or to just get a little something for their breakfast amidst their busy comings and goings. When the commotion finally settled, Mariah sat at one of the little tables, watching tiny snowflakes drift slowly down from low-hanging clouds to the cobbled street, where they accumulated like a sprinkling of sugar over freshly baked biscuits. She looked up into the clouds as if she might be able to see the source of such beautiful wonder floating down from heaven. But she saw nothing but the usual vague, dingy white foggy clouds that rarely lifted their blanketing effect over London. Becoming entranced by the little snowflakes, it occurred to her that Christmas was now less than a month away.

The bakery was always busier for the holiday, with special orders of puddings and cakes and delicacies for the parties and celebrations that would take place in many fine households. They would celebrate Christmas as usual here in their home—which was above the bakery and accessed by stairs near the back door. There would be no extravagance or luxury in their celebrations, but it would be filled with meaning and joy as it always had been, thanks to her father. He was simply the kind of man who understood the truest meaning of Christmas, and he showed it in the way he lived his life every day of the year. Mariah thought of how there was no better example of Christian living than Matthew Pritchard, and she smiled to think of the inevitable fun she would share with her father and brother in the coming weeks as they prepared for this holiday of holidays, gathering together for their own version of a Christmas feast and the exchanging of surprise gifts that would be kept delightfully secret until Christmas morning.

Mariah knew that many people didn't take Christmas as seriously as they did. Some only saw it as an excuse for parties and indulging in more of the lavishness that came with their wealth and privilege. Mariah couldn't begrudge them too much when their desire for fancy baked goods in abundance helped the bakery thrive. But she felt sad on their behalf, wishing they could go about their celebrations with a better understanding of the reason for the holiday and all it represented. Then there were the poor and destitute who had no means or purpose in celebrating anything. Mariah once again forced away her thoughts of them, wishing she could do more but knowing that she couldn't. But there were all of the people between the poor and the rich, those who lived comfortable lives, many of whom simply chose not to make too much of a fuss over Christmas. And Mariah just didn't understand. To her, it was a magical time of year, a holiday filled with hope and promise. She wished that the sprinkling of tiny snowflakes could spread the cheer she felt to all who had it come down upon their heads. Knowing she could only truly control her own attitude, Mariah began to hum a familiar Christmas carol while she focused her attention more fully on the beauty of the gentle snowfall, feeling a magical anticipation bubbling inside of her while in her mind she planned the gifts that she would give to her father and brother.

"You seem happy," her father said, startling her slightly as he sat down on the chair across the table from her.

"Why shouldn't I be?" she asked. "Isn't the snow beautiful?"

"It is indeed," Matthew said with enthusiasm and, of course, a smile.

"I was thinking about Christmas. It's my favorite time of year, you know."

"Yes, I know," her father said. "You get that from me, I think. It's our *busiest* time of year," he added, "but as I've said before, I think that adds to the charm."

"And I've been around long enough to know that you're right."

"Is everything all right?" he asked, and she turned to him in surprise, noting a hint of a scowl.

"Yes, of course," she insisted, curious over such a question when he'd just commented on her seeming happy. "Why do you ask?"

"You just seemed . . . down when you came in earlier."

Mariah turned her attention back to the snow and tried to shake off the memories of cold and hungry people huddling in alleys. She only said, "Just the usual. I'll be fine."

"You know we would do more if we could," Matthew said, setting his hand over hers where it rested on the table.

"I know," she said and gave him a convincing smile that seemed to assure him that she was all right, his scowl having disappeared.

"Perhaps we could make some special treats to pass out on Christmas morning along with the usual bread," he suggested.

"That's an excellent idea," she said, liking it very much. In the enormous, incomprehensible perspective of the entire world—or even just the city of London—with all its suffering and hardship, offering a little Christmas biscuit sprinkled with sugar hardly seemed like it would make a difference. But it might—if only in reminding people that God was surely mindful of their suffering and that a better life existed beyond this one, all thanks to the Savior whom the Christmas season honored. As that thought settled into her, she added with enthusiasm, "Perhaps we could wrap the extra treats up like a little gift and tie a note to each one that might offer a message of hope and peace, just to remind these people that it *is* Christmas and that there is hope for something better."

Matthew's smile broadened—which made it fill his entire face. "That's my girl!" he said. "What an excellent idea! You have so much of your mother in you."

"I thought I was like you," she said.

"In some ways." He tipped his head with a nostalgic chuckle. "But she always came up with such lovely ideas for simple ways that we could do good for others. She believed so strongly in the principle that as we continually gave to those in need from the abundance we were given, we would be richly blessed in return. And we always have been. You carry on her beliefs very well, my dear, and it makes me proud of you."

Mariah just smiled at her father and looked again at the falling snow, now even more excited for Christmas. She would go and purchase paper and ribbon later today so they could get busy figuring out the proper message and writing it on individual notes. On Christmas they would not only plan on more than the usual pieces of bread they distributed; they would make an extra effort to walk farther and find those who might need just a simple offering of love and hope. In that moment she felt certain this could very well be the best Christmas of her life.

CHAPTER 2
The Beggar

JOSEPH TREADMORE TUGGED HIS HAT down over the tops of his ears and wrapped his muffler around the lower half of his face in order to endure his walk through the stinging cold to get to his place of employment. He tried his best to just keep his eyes focused on where he was going, as opposed to actually looking around where he knew from experience he would only see signs of suffering and poverty. He hated the helplessness he felt, especially when he was living so close to the edge of barely being able to meet his own needs. He knew it would only take one tiny unforeseen incident to push him over the cliff into joining those who had nothing and nowhere to go. He wondered how many of these people lived this kind of life simply because an injury or illness had prevented them from being able to work for their meager living and subsequently they'd been left with nothing at all. Given his upbringing he felt completely separate from the people he passed in the streets in this part of London where the wealthy and powerful never set foot. But living among them had made him feel like he understood them—or at least he was trying to. And he prayed every day that he would never be faced with crossing that line into such helplessness and hopelessness. He was grateful to be able to work for his living—even if the only employment he'd been able to find barely afforded him a cramped room in the attic of a boardinghouse and the means to purchase enough food to keep him alive and able to work. He believed he would rather die than be condemned to live on the streets and beg, but he assumed the people living that way probably felt the same. Death surely seemed a preferable option over the many things in the world of such wretchedness and affliction.

Joseph became pleasantly distracted from his dismal thoughts when he saw a woman walking toward him, too bundled up against the cold for him to see anything but her face. But oh, such a beautiful face! Her smile seemed to permeate the atmosphere around her and brightened everything that was otherwise gloomy beneath the typical cover of fog and soot in the air. He slowed his pace just to watch her for a long moment as he realized she was passing out small rounds of bread to the beggars and those who were too cold or weak to even have the strength to beg. He realized then that he'd seen this woman before—maybe two or three times—but he'd been too caught up in his own thoughts to really pay attention. He slowed down to the point when he was barely walking, fascinated with the way weary faces would light up as poverty-stricken hands reached out to accept her humble offering. It was as if in that very moment she was easing the pain and sorrow that had been so glumly occupying his mind.

Joseph didn't realize he'd *stopped* walking and that he was actually staring at this woman, until he realized she was looking back at him. And then she was holding what seemed the bread of life toward him with a dainty gloved hand. She smiled at him, but there was sadness in her eyes, as if she too was overcome by the same helplessness he'd been feeling.

"No . . . thank you," he said, holding up his hands. "You're very kind, but . . . I had some breakfast. You should give it to someone who needs it more than I do." She nodded and withdrew the offering, but she didn't look away. Nervously attempting to fill the silence—since he didn't want her to go—he muttered, "I'm blessed to be able to work for my living. Your generosity toward those who are not so fortunate has touched me . . . and lifted my spirits. Thank you."

Her smile actually broadened, which he didn't think possible. And was that a glisten of tears he saw in her eyes? "You're very kind, sir," she said, and the melodic effect of her voice added a layer of charm to her brilliant countenance. She was like an angel of hope standing there in the middle of all things gloomy and harsh. "I wish you a good day," she added and then seemed to become aware that they both had somewhere they needed to be going.

"And you," he said and watched her walk away for a lengthy moment before he forced himself back to the present and the absolute need to not be late. He had to run a little to make up for his brief respite with the bread lady, but his heart felt lighter and the day before him didn't seem nearly as tedious and dismal.

Joseph arrived at the livery just as the clock was chiming the hour, and he was relieved to have made it on time. Mr. Dowd—his employer and the owner of Dowd's Livery—barely acknowledged him with a cursory glance. He then glanced at the clock, as if to silently make it known that he was keeping track of whether or not Joseph might be arriving late. Joseph disliked his employer immensely; he was cranky and terse and all-around miserable— which reminded Joseph a little too much of his father. But Joseph was grateful for work, even if it was a lowly job that paid very little. Given that he had absolutely no skills in any form of labor, finding employment had been much more difficult than he'd anticipated, and he'd quickly run out of what little money he'd had with him when he'd left home. The entire experience of all that had preceded his leaving—and the absolute humbling impact of all he'd endured since—had changed him deeply, or perhaps it had helped him understand who he really was and why. Now, he was simply grateful that Mr. Dowd had been willing to give him a job, and he was determined to work hard and never give this man any doubt as to whether or not Joseph had earned every shilling.

Joseph spent the day mucking out stables and feeding and caring for horses. He didn't mind the work when he was left alone to do it, but he wasn't terribly fond of having Mr. Dowd around. Unfortunately, his employer felt the need to check in frequently with Joseph to make certain he was doing everything perfectly according to his strict specifications. Given the months Joseph had been working there and the fact that Mr. Dowd hadn't noticed a single problem after the first week, the man's lack of trust and respect felt demeaning to Joseph. But he just did his job and kept his opinions to himself, reminding himself often of his gratitude for having a roof over his head and food to eat.

Throughout the day Joseph thought often of the bread lady, and thoughts of her always provoked a smile—almost against his will. He wished they'd had more time to talk; he ached for human interaction and real conversation. But he'd not found anyone since he'd left home that he actually wanted to talk to more than polite greetings and trivial exchanges. He found himself imagining crossing her path again—perhaps on his way home so that he wouldn't be in such a hurry. And they could talk; he didn't care *what* they talked about. He just wanted someone to talk to, and instinctively he believed—even from their very brief encounter—that she was a person capable of good, sound conversation. He began to wonder where she lived and worked, and he concluded with obviousness that she worked in a bakery. There had been too much fresh bread in her basket to have been baked in the average kitchen in this part of town. He assessed that there weren't very many bakeries between where he worked and where he lived; in fact, he'd purchased bread for himself many times on his way home from work. But he'd never seen *her* at the bakery he went to. He considered searching out other bakeries so that perhaps he could find her. But to what end? By the time his work day ended, he'd talked himself out of it, knowing he was deluding himself to think that such an obviously fine woman would find any interest in a man like him—even if all he really wanted was someone to talk to.

Over the next week or so, Joseph watched closely for the bread lady on his way to work. He started leaving home a little earlier so that he could walk more slowly or even hesitate discreetly somewhere until he saw her. He maneuvered casually passing by her just so he could see her smile and hear her tell him hello. He said hello or good day in return and kept walking, not wanting to seem presumptuous—or worse, cause her any alarm. Crime was prevalent in the area, and he wouldn't want her to think some strange man had taken an inappropriate interest in her. His motives were noble, but she wouldn't know that. So, he simply enjoyed her smiles and her simple greetings, and he enjoyed discreetly observing as she passed out her daily offerings of manna to the hungry.

Joseph was surprised to see her on the street engaged in her usual task on Sunday morning as well. Nearly every business closed on Sundays, except for those that were absolutely necessary. The livery was one of those exceptions, since travelers came through every day of the week and horses needed to be cared for whether they were just passing through or being kept in the livery for longer periods of time. Joseph didn't really mind since he had stopped going to church long before he'd left home, and being with the horses had a calming effect. They needed to eat and drink every day of the week—just as people did. And he was glad to be able to do that for these fine creatures. But Joseph knew bakeries were closed on Sundays. People had to plan ahead and buy extra baked goods on Saturday. So it naturally surprised him when the bread lady was out and about with her basket of offerings on an extremely cold Sunday morning. Of course, being hungry was a constant element of the human condition, and it never took a day off. Joseph watched her discreetly from behind an awning post and thought of a story in the Bible about Jesus healing a man on the Sabbath. His prior thoughts about her being an angel amplified in his mind. She was truly precious.

The following day Joseph *did* go to a different bakery on his way home from work, but there was an old woman there who was talkative enough to let him know that she only had her grandson working with her there. The day after that he went to a place called Pritchard's Bake Shoppe, where he purchased two soft buns to eat on his way home. He was helped by a boy who looked too young to be left in charge of a bake shop, but he was polite and efficient and kind. Unfortunately he wasn't at all talkative, so Joseph wasn't able to ascertain if the woman he hoped to find might work there. As he walked back out onto the already darkened streets, he figured it might be just as well. His curiosity was likely better left alone. Without really knowing her, he could imagine her to be anything he liked, and he didn't have to wonder if she might find him dull or disappointing. Given that he had trouble not believing he was a disappointment to everyone who had ever known him, remaining aloof seemed a better option.

Joseph ate the buns as he walked, being careful not to bump into anyone walking the other direction. They tasted immensely good and satisfied him both in body and spirit. He also felt satisfied to know that his week's pay was safely tucked into his pocket. He could pay another week's rent and divvy up the rest for his daily meals. Another week of surviving and not crossing over the edge into the wretchedness of a life that was far too close for comfort.

Joseph was almost to the boardinghouse where he lived when a strange noise from behind caught him off guard and put his senses on alert. But before he could think of what the problem might be, he was hit over the back of the head, and he fell hard onto the ground, only to be hit several more times by more than one man, with not even a tiny chance of being able to defend himself. Barely holding onto consciousness and brutally aware of a great deal of pain, Joseph became aware that his pockets were being searched and his chest tightened with a different kind of pain to realize he'd just been robbed of his week's wages. He now had no money for his rent, no money for food, and he was injured too seriously to even get up and walk. He prayed silently for mercy, secretly hoping that God's mercy would bring death as a welcome relief. There were things worse than death; he knew that. And the prospect of living among the freezing beggars on the street certainly fit into that category.

～∾

Mariah checked on Mattie to make certain he'd eaten his breakfast and he was doing his chores before she removed her apron and began bundling up to go outside for the usual morning rounds in the streets. Freshly baked goods had already been set out in the store front, and the ovens were busily engaged in baking the next batch, with another set of buns now rising while they waited their turn. With her father left to watch over the baking and Mattie all ready to help customers as they came in, Mariah set out with the usual basket of bread on her arm. There was an extra bite in the air as she set out, and she felt a pang of concern for those who had had no choice but to spend the night outside. In such moments she wished for great wealth; for herself, she had everything she could ever need or want, but she wanted desperately to have the resources to help these people. While she walked she imagined having an enormous home where she could invite dozens of cold and hungry people to stay beneath her roof and find relief. She imagined assigning everyone tasks according to their abilities to help keep the household functioning so that all would earn their keep for the sake of their own dignity and self-respect. It was a fantasy she loved to indulge in, but the reality of limited resources always brought her mind back to the cold streets of London, where pinched and weary faces offered her wan smiles and heartfelt thank-yous as they received her humble offering.

With Mariah's basket empty, she headed back toward home, habitually glancing down each alleyway she passed to make certain she hadn't missed anyone. Even though she had no more bread with her, she was willing to go back to the bakery and get more if she found anyone else who needed some nourishment. She'd come to know most of the people who haunted the area and the places they had chosen that had in a sense become their own, the spot where they huddled at night to best avoid the wind. She saw an unfamiliar form, huddled in a nearly indiscernible mass on the ground against the aging brick wall of a building. Her heart quickened as she approached, sensing that something was terribly wrong. Having spent years doing what she did each day, she had more than once found a person dead from illness combined with exposure to the elements, and she'd had to send for the local constable. Those memories haunted her, and she certainly didn't want to experience such a thing again. She approached tentatively and crouched down enough to get a better look at this man. His head was on the ground and one arm partially covered his face, but she could immediately see evidence that he was hurt. *Beaten?* It appeared that way.

"Lord, have mercy," she murmured and gently moved his arm, fearing she would find him dead. But he groaned and his eyes flickered open slightly. She recognized him then; she'd passed this man many times on the street. She'd once offered him bread, but he'd told her he had employment, that he could care for himself and her offering should be given to someone who needed it more. She'd been touched by his kindness and humility, and she'd been fascinated by his eyes and his smile. She'd found herself watching for him each morning and had been disappointed on the days when their paths hadn't crossed. And now he was here, freezing and hurt very badly; the exact severity of his injuries was impossible to determine. She needed to help him, and now. But she couldn't do it alone.

"I'll be right back," she said gently, touching his face to let him know he wasn't hallucinating.

Mariah hurried back to the street, praying for guidance as she went. She only stood there for a moment before she saw a young man she knew who was the milliner's son. "Bob!" she called, and he turned. "I need your help!" The boy hurried her direction with an expression that let her know he would be glad to do whatever she asked of him. That was the blessing of having good neighbors and camaraderie in the community. "A man has been badly hurt. I need to get him out of the cold." She quickly assessed Bob's maturing stature and added, "Do you think you can help me get him to the bakery?"

"O' course," Bob said eagerly and followed her into the alley.

"I'll send for the doctor," Mariah explained to Bob, thinking aloud. "But first we must get him warm."

"O' course," Bob said again, now looking down at the injured man. "Poor ol' soul. Looks pretty roughed up."

"How badly are you hurt?" Mariah asked the man, again touching his face to make him more aware of her presence. "Do you think you can stand and walk with our help? We need to get you someplace warm."

∽≈∾

Joseph attempted to blink away the unnatural sleepiness that had come over him after lying here in the cold for seemingly endless hours. He turned slightly toward the woman speaking to him. He'd been imagining this angel of mercy finding him, only because he knew her morning route of scouring the streets for the destitute and ailing. Still, he'd not fully believed it would happen—as if he were somehow unworthy of such a miracle, or perhaps he'd feared his injuries would leave him dead before the light of day. But here she was, and for the first time since he'd been assaulted the previous evening he had a glimmer of hope that he might actually live beyond this. There were many challenges beyond simply remaining alive, but for the moment that's all he could think about.

"Sir?" the woman said. "Can you hear me? Do you think you can stand and—"

"I think so," Joseph said, noticing a strong young man standing above him as well.

"This is Bob," the woman said. "We're going to do our best to get you back to the bakery where you can get warm, and I'll send for the doctor."

Joseph wanted to protest against having her do so much for him, but he couldn't find the presence of mind or the will of spirit to do anything but attempt to stand with their help. For now he simply focused on his gratitude, thinking he'd find a way to make it up to her. Bob proved to be very strong indeed as he hoisted Joseph to his feet and helped him assess that he could indeed stand and walk as long as Bob kept a firm arm around him. Joseph's pain was more in his head and his middle than in his legs. The only problem with walking was that his limbs felt numb from the cold, but after a few unsteady steps he managed to get his footing. The bread lady guided his arm around her shoulders, and she helped support him from the other side while she and Bob guided him out of the alley onto the street and toward the bakery. He wasn't at all sure *which* bakery she hailed from, and since they took him down another alley and through a back door, he still didn't know.

Joseph was helped onto a chair while he heard the woman say to Bob, "Go and get my father from the kitchen, please."

Bob hurried away and was back in what seemed seconds with an older man who Joseph couldn't see clearly, but his voice was kind. "Lord, have mercy," he said almost exactly the way the woman had said it when she'd first found him. "Let's take him up to Mattie's bed, and Mattie can share my room for now. He needs a—"

"I'll go for the doctor," Bob offered eagerly.

"We can send Mattie," the woman said, "if there's somewhere you need to be."

"I gots time," Bob said.

"Oh, thank you," the woman said. "When you come back, get yourself something from the kitchen."

"I won't say no to that," Bob said with a chuckle. "I'll hurry," he added more seriously and left.

Joseph felt himself being hoisted to his feet again by the woman and her father. "Can you make it up the stairs?" the man asked.

"I think so," Joseph said and felt the woman guide his hand to the stair rail that was attached to the wall. They slowly ascended a dark, narrow staircase, and he was guided into a small bedroom with a big window where the light of a cloudy London morning filtrated in, which made it easier for him to see.

Joseph was led to the edge of the bed, the father making certain he was able to sit before he let go of him. "You're far too kind," Joseph said, humbled and grateful beyond words. "I'll find a way to repay you and—"

"There's no need to be concerned about such things right now," the man said with a depth of kindness that allowed Joseph to catch a glimpse of where the bread lady had gotten her generous spirit. The man turned to his daughter, who was standing nearby wringing her hands and biting her lip with overt concern. Her father said to her, "You take care of things downstairs, my dear, and I'll help him get comfortable and cleaned up a bit before the doctor gets here."

"I'll bring some warm water," the woman said. "Let me know if you need anything else."

Joseph's humility deepened when this man knelt on the floor to remove Joseph's shoes, saying gently, "We must get your feet and hands warmed up first thing." Joseph wanted to say that it sounded like this man had some experience, but before he could, the man added, "You're not the first we've brought into our home in need of warmth and care." He chuckled as if he found the idea pleasant rather than a burden. "I do believe I'm getting rather good at this." He smiled at Joseph. "I'm Matthew Pritchard. You may call me Matthew—we don't stand on ceremony here."

If his generous host wanted Joseph to be on Christian-name terms with him, Joseph felt the least he could do to repay the man was extend the same courtesy. "Joseph" was the only word he could get out, feeling light-headed and foggy.

"A pleasure to meet you, Joseph. I don't want you to worry about anything right now except getting yourself healed and strong. We'll take care of the rest."

"I'm . . . grateful," Joseph managed.

While Matthew removed Joseph's shoes and stockings and coat, he told him that he had a young son named after himself. Matthew talked about his son with pride over how maturely he served the customers in the bakery and that he was such a good lad. Joseph perked up a little as Matthew told him about his daughter, Mariah. *Mariah.* Joseph took that in. Her name was Mariah. He was glad to be able to stop thinking of her as the bread lady.

Matthew continued helping Joseph get out of his dirty clothes and into the warm bed while he talked about Mariah with the same admiration he'd expressed in regard to Mattie. He told Joseph she was kind and good to the core, but Joseph already knew that. Matthew stoked the fire in the room then used a clean rag and warm water to attempt to clean the dried blood from the cuts on Joseph's lip, cheek, and eyebrow. Joseph winced more than once, and Matthew apologized, but he kept talking about his bakery and his children as if talking might keep Joseph distracted—which it did.

Before the doctor arrived, Joseph already felt better. He was incredibly sore, but he was starting to warm up. He couldn't think about the fact that he no longer had rent money or a job; Mr. Dowd would have terminated his employment within minutes of his not showing up for work. He was grateful for these people and didn't want to think about what might have happened to him if they'd not been so generous. But once he healed he had to be on his way, and he would have to find another job and somewhere to live—again. He chose not to think about that now; instead he focused on his gratitude and the warmth permeating his body. It was almost painful at first to have his freezing nerves take in the heat of the surrounding room, but then it felt so good that he knew heaven was surely a place of such pleasant warmth.

The doctor arrived and kindly asked Joseph many questions about what had happened and where he'd been hurt. Being warmer allowed Joseph to think more clearly, and he was able to tell the doctor everything. Matthew hovered in the room, as visibly concerned as he might have been if Joseph were someone he actually knew and cared about. The doctor checked Joseph thoroughly and declared that he had some nasty cuts and bruises but nothing that wouldn't heal with time. He gave Matthew two different remedies in small jars—one to be applied to the cuts, and the other for the bruises, which were mostly on Joseph's torso.

As soon as the doctor left, Matthew sat on the edge of the bed to help apply the doctor's remedies. Joseph muttered, "You don't need to do this. Surely I can manage."

"Perhaps," Matthew said and urged Joseph to sit up so that he could gently rub liniment on his bruised back, "but I doubt you could reach back here, and I know you're weak."

"I can't argue with that," Joseph said and felt the need to add, "I'll find a way to repay you for the doctor's fee and for—"

"Now, stop that, young man," Matthew said, urging Joseph to relax against the pillows beneath his head. "The doctor enjoys our baked goods for payment, and he's a kind and generous man. Just get yourself stronger. You'll feel better in a few days."

"I don't know what to say," Joseph muttered, suddenly exhausted. He hadn't slept a moment through the night, cold and hurting in the alley, terrified that some other thug would come along and finish him off.

"No need to say anything," Matthew insisted. "Rest for a bit, and we'll get you something to eat as soon as the rush has settled somewhat."

"Thank you," Joseph said and fell asleep within moments after Matthew had left the room and closed the door.

CHAPTER 3
Angel of Hope

JOSEPH AWOKE TO A PLEASANT aroma and the voice of a boy saying, "Sorry to be disturbing you, sir, but my father said that it was about time you should be having something to eat." Joseph realized it was dark outside and more than one lamp was burning in the room. "You slept for hours; you must have been very tired."

Joseph forced his eyes to focus on this boy, whose features were so remarkably like his father's that there was no question to whom he belonged. "You must be Mattie," Joseph said and sat up, only to be immediately reminded of his many injuries and the need to move slowly.

"Let me help you, sir," Mattie said after setting a tray of food on the little bureau nearby. The boy rushed to put pillows against the headboard and then firmly took hold of Joseph's upper arm to help him get situated. Mattie's scrawny appearance was deceptive, as he proved to have a great deal of strength, which Joseph appreciated more than he wanted to admit.

"Thank you," Joseph said and managed to get as comfortable as possible given the aching in his head and much of his body.

"A pleasure, sir," Mattie said.

"You must stop that," Joseph said as Mattie put the tray over Joseph's lap. Mattie looked alarmed, and Joseph added, "You must stop calling me sir. My name is Joseph, and I know that I'm currently occupying your bed so you should know I'm very grateful to you."

"It's not a problem . . . Joseph." Mattie smiled, and Joseph saw evidence that he was also related by blood to the bread lady. Mariah; her name was Mariah. "We've done this sort of thing plenty of times. I don't mind sleeping in with Papa; he tells me stories until I fall asleep—like he did when I was a youngster." He said it as if he were now an adult, which made Joseph smile.

"Is there anything else I can get for you?" Mattie asked, nodding toward the food.

"I'm more than all right," Joseph said. "Thank you."

Mattie left the room, and Joseph began to eat. He was glad to be alone when he realized how ravenously hungry he was, and it was the best-tasting food he'd eaten since before he'd left home. Or perhaps ever. After devouring every crumb, he managed to get out of bed as long as he moved slowly. He took advantage of the clean water that had been left in the room, and freshened up. Examining his face in a small mirror on the wall, he understood why it hurt so much, but he again counted himself very blessed to be alive and to have been taken in by such good people.

Matthew came in a short while later to make certain that Joseph had everything he needed. They chatted a little while Matthew helped apply the doctor's remedies and saw that he was set for the night. Matthew then declared that bedtime came early in their household, given that they all had to be up long before the sun in order to have fresh baked goods ready and waiting before customers came to the bakery for their morning purchases.

"Thank you . . . for everything," Joseph said and was left alone. The loneliness wasn't unfamiliar, but the sense of comfort and security—and kindness he'd been offered—felt strangely uncomfortable yet soothing at the same time. Even when he'd lived in a fine household with many servants, he'd never felt as cared for as he did now.

Given how much he'd slept through the day, Joseph didn't expect to be able to sleep again so soon, but he crawled into bed anyway, and once he'd managed to get himself as comfortable as possible, he drifted off and woke only a couple of times in the night when shifting his position had caused pain. But he'd quickly gone back to sleep both times and awoke to sunlight peering between the nearly closed curtains and the consoling aroma of freshly baked bread mingled with that of other unknown delicacies. His efforts to sit up in bed were much easier than they had been the day before, and he immediately realized that someone had been in the room because the room was warm from the blazing fire, fresh water was in the basin on the washstand, and the clothes he'd been wearing when he'd been found in the alley were spread over the footboard of the bed—clean and mended. There was also a clean nightshirt there, which he assumed belonged to Matthew and was meant to replace the one he had loaned Joseph upon his arrival. He considered the clean nightshirt an invitation to stay here for at least another night or two, but he had to figure out what to do beyond that, which meant that he needed to get himself out of bed and work on finding a position.

It took Joseph a terribly long time to get dressed, but he managed, all the while wondering what he would do now. These people had saved his life and offered much kindness, but he had to figure out a way to provide for himself and somehow recover from this setback. He tried not to feel depressed over the absolute helplessness he felt when he recalled how difficult it had been to simply find any employment at all. As much as he would not miss Mr. Dowd, he'd needed the work. But that opportunity was lost to him now, and he had to find the determination to start over.

All dressed except for his boots, Joseph sat on the edge of the bed and looked at them with trepidation, completely worn out from the effort it had taken to get this far. A knock at the door startled him, but he called, "Come in."

He was more pleased than he would ever dare admit to see Mariah come into the room with a tray. She took one look at him and declared with chagrin, "You shouldn't be trying to get up and about in your condition!"

"I'm doing much better," he insisted and watched her set the tray down, after which she turned again to face him, her hands on her hips, her expression betraying how much she'd been a mother figure to her little brother.

"It's impressive that you've managed to dress yourself, sir," she said with mild indignation, "but I'd wager you can't get down the stairs on your own." She picked up his boots and set them in a far corner of the room while she added, "So get yourself back into that bed and get the rest you need so you can heal properly."

Joseph chuckled even while he scooted carefully back onto the bed to lean against the headboard and the pillows there.

"You find this amusing?" she asked, setting the tray over his lap.

He wanted to tell her that he found her *very* amusing, but he didn't want to be misunderstood. It was more accurate that he was utterly and completely fascinated with her, but to try and explain that might sound even more disrespectful when they barely knew each other. He settled for saying, "I find it refreshing to have someone actually care about my well being." He hoped she heard the gratitude he'd intended in the statement.

Mariah looked a little taken aback, but a moment later he realized she was staring at him with some kind of intrigue sparkling in her eyes. His heart quickened as he considered that she might be as fascinated with him as he was with her. The idea seemed impossible and preposterous. But what he saw in her eyes couldn't be ignored. When she realized she was staring she cleared her throat and looked away. He expected her to act embarrassed or rush from the room—or both—but she sat on the edge of the bed and looked at him again, although this time her eyes were more guarded.

"I'm Mariah," she said.

"Yes, I know. Your father and brother have been very forthcoming."

"Of course." She laughed softly, and he loved the sound of it. "And you're Joseph. I'm afraid that's all I know about you, which puts me at a disadvantage. My father and brother have both told me that you've been very kind and polite but you've said nothing about yourself—or how you landed in the situation in which I found you."

"It's a long story," he said, not wanting to talk about it—at all. "And likely a very boring one."

He was afraid she'd push him to talk about himself and was relieved when she didn't. Although he wasn't necessarily pleased when she said instead, "I assume you have nowhere to go, or—"

"No," he interrupted her, wanting to say it himself. He owed these people an explanation, and it needed to be truthful. "I was working for Mr. Dowd at the livery." Her expression soured slightly, and he felt certain she knew Mr. Dowd—or at least his reputation. "I was renting a room, but since my rent was due and my week's wages were stolen, I'm certain that what little I owned that was left there is long gone." He hurried to add what he knew was most important. "But as soon as I'm healed, I will find work and be on my way. I'm grateful beyond words for your kindness, but I will not become a burden to you and your family. You need to know that."

"I can assure you," she said, "that we would never let you or anyone else become a burden. My father is a generous soul, but he also expects a person to earn their keep and do the work they're capable of doing." Joseph was glad to hear that but surprised when she added, "And right now you're not capable of doing anything but healing, and you will offend my father's generosity if you don't give yourself the time to heal properly. When you're up to it, he will gladly find work for you to do here until you can find employment elsewhere, so you needn't worry about that. We can't afford to pay anyone wages, but we can give you a place to sleep and food to eat. For now, that's all you need to think about."

Joseph felt a sudden urge to cry—something he hadn't allowed himself to do since he'd initially left home. Her absolute kindness—and that of her father and brother—filled him with a warmth he'd never experienced before. The very lack of fear and worry she'd just offered him was such a deep relief that he could hardly take it in. Without even realizing it, Mariah had just given him something he'd not felt in a very long time; something he knew was in short supply among the people in this world who were just struggling to survive. *Hope.* The same way she passed out bread to the hungry, she had just given him the ability to believe that life could actually get better and there was something worth living for.

⤳〜⤵

Mariah hurried out of the room their wounded guest was using and closed the door, hoping he hadn't noticed the abruptness of her exit. She'd looked into his eyes more times than she could count as they'd passed each other on the street, and she'd always been affected—even if she'd never been able to define exactly why. But she'd never imagined the possibility that he would end up living here in her own home, in need of their assistance and care until he was able to heal and regain his independence. He was far from the first man they'd brought into their home under similar circumstances, but he was certainly the first and only man she'd ever encountered anywhere who held this strange power over her.

Mariah went quickly back downstairs and got busy doing her usual work, trying without success to keep Joseph out of her mind. She knew absolutely nothing about him—nothing beyond his given name and the fact that he was polite and kind and humble. Although, she couldn't deny that she knew enough to believe he was genuine in the way he portrayed himself. Instinctively she knew he was a man of integrity. She'd had some hard lessons in the past when she'd naively believed that every person they had tried to help would return their assistance with gratitude and honesty. They had been robbed and treated badly by at least a few of the people they had brought into their home. Mariah had initially become very mistrusting of *all* people, but her father had patiently helped both her and Mattie understand that many people simply didn't know how to be honest, and they lived in too much fear to be able to live any other way. Matthew's own generous heart had not been damaged by the bad behavior of the few, but rather he continued to assume that all people in need had goodness in their hearts, and no matter their circumstances or intentions, all men and women were children of God and it was their duty to be kind and giving. Mariah had learned through her father's tutelage and her own diligent prayer over the matter how to be discerning of the characters of people she encountered. Over time she'd been blessed with an ability to almost literally see the light in people's eyes—or the absence of it. Her ability hadn't changed her willingness to give aid to anyone she encountered who might be in need, but it had helped her know when she needed to be cautious in order to protect herself and her home and family. If she'd believed Joseph was the kind of man to return their kindness with any sort of ill will, she still would have helped him—but they would have made other arrangements to give him aid once he was able to get up and about. Her father had made it clear to her and Mattie that he wanted Joseph to have an opportunity to work in the bakery—at least for the time being—and to see how that transpired. He'd given Mariah the assignment to let Joseph know it was an option for him. But Mariah hadn't been prepared for the sparkle of relief and gratitude she'd seen in his eyes or the way his entire countenance had practically glowed with humility and . . . something else—something she couldn't define, but it made her feel warm from the inside out every time she thought about him.

CHAPTER 4
A Warm Kitchen

THE DAY WAS TYPICALLY VERY busy, and Mariah made certain that she sent Mattie to check on Joseph and see that he had all he needed. She wanted to see him again and at the same time felt terrified to be in the same room with him—or perhaps more accurately, she was terrified of the way he made her feel. Long past the usual time she went to bed, she sat in the parlor of their home above the bakery and looked into the glowing coals of the fire, wondering if what she felt could possibly be what she both hoped and feared it might be. She'd heard her father tell the story many times of how he'd known almost instantly that her mother was the love of his life. She gasped aloud to realize she had been comparing thoughts of Joseph to the way her parents had felt about each other. She needed to check her thoughts and be more careful not to allow her feelings to get completely out of hand.

"Is something wrong?" Matthew said and startled her; she hadn't realized he was in the room. When she didn't answer, he added, "I heard you gasp. What are you thinking about?"

Mariah was still trying to gather her words even after her father had scooted a chair close to her and sat down. She knew better than to try and skirt around the truth of her thoughts and feelings. Matthew Pritchard was a perceptive man—almost to a fault. He could sell bread to a customer and gauge their mood immediately, and he was keenly skilled at being able to make kind inquiries and let people know that he sincerely cared about the challenges in their lives, both large and small. Mariah suspected that people came to their bakery in need of her father's kindness every bit as much as their need for his quality baked goods. But Matthew was most perceptive about his children's moods—surely because he knew them better than anyone. And Mariah would be a fool to think her father hadn't noticed how preoccupied with her thoughts she'd been all day.

"You know," Matthew said, taking Mariah's hand, "you're never going to make sense of the way you feel if you keep sending your brother to help Joseph."

Mariah gasped again and shot her father an astonished glare. As much as she knew his perceptive nature, she was taken off guard by his succinct and perfectly accurate summation of the problem. Before she could speak, he smiled at her and added, "Do you think I wouldn't notice that you've been entirely different since the moment he came through our door?" Mariah turned to look into the flames, still unable to come up with anything to say. She was glad when he continued to speak, hoping he might be able to offer some of the sound wisdom and insight she so desperately needed. "I've never seen you like this," he added, his tone more gentle. "There have been men who have caught your attention over the years. I know you've been attracted to more than a few, and you've had some disappointments. But dare I say that you've never felt this way before?"

Mariah finally spoke. "Why would you say that?" Matthew just smiled at her again and looked back at the fire, as if to declare that he'd opened the door for her to share her feelings and he expected her to do so. "Well . . . you're right. I haven't ever felt this way before . . . and I don't know why. Anything I've ever felt in the past seems trite and silly in comparison, and yet . . . I don't understand how that's possible, when I don't even know him."

"Don't you?" Matthew asked with an intensity in his eyes that caught her attention. "You may not know much *about* him, but I think you *know* him very well. You're a sharp and discerning woman, Mariah. You have good common sense, and you need to pay attention to it. But you also have an open and sensitive heart, and you need to pay attention to that as well. Don't ignore one or the other, and don't allow one to suppress the other. You need both your mind and your heart to know what's right. But Mariah, my dearest," Matthew took her hand and looked into her eyes, "you need to at least consider the possibility that the reason you've never felt this way before is because you've never met anyone like him—and maybe you never will again. I know you better than to think you might do anything rash or foolish; my concern is actually quite the opposite."

"What do you mean?" she asked, wondering if such a comment had been some kind of criticism.

"What I mean," Matthew continued kindly, "is that I'm more concerned that you might do *nothing* out of some kind of fear of being rash or foolish. But you are neither of those things. I think he's going to be around for a while, so get to know him better. There's no harm in that. Follow your heart, my dear."

Mariah sat in silence for several minutes, just taking in everything her father had said, and was consoled to note that it settled in very comfortably. She wanted very much to ask her father a question that seemed silly given that she knew the answer; he'd told the story dozens of times. But she wanted to hear it again, even though she knew that her bringing it up now would leave him with absolutely no doubt about how she was feeling. She finally worked up the nerve and just said it. "Tell me again how you knew Mother was the right one for you."

Matthew chuckled softly and surprised her with his answer. "You don't need me to tell you that right now. You already know that I saw something special in her the first time our eyes met, and it was only a matter of days before I knew we could make each other happy and we could make a good life together. I asked her to marry me less than a month after I met her, and I knew it was right. I have no regrets, Mariah, but I must confess that I have often thought of how I almost talked myself out of pursuing her because it seemed so illogical that I could feel that way about her so quickly. If I *had* talked myself out of it, *that* would have been my biggest regret."

Mariah turned more toward her father, noting the familiar dreamy look in his eyes that always appeared when he spoke of her mother. "But how can you *know* such things, Father?"

Matthew looked a little surprised by the question, as if she'd just asked him how to make bread, when it was something he'd taught her many years ago and she was perfectly capable of doing it well without any help whatsoever from him. But he answered firmly, "You just know, Mariah. You know it like you know God exists even though you can't prove it. You just know."

Matthew stood and kissed her on the forehead. "You should get some sleep, my dear. It's not so many hours until the ovens need to be hot and ready."

Mariah knew he was right, but she also knew that attempting to sleep right now would be pointless. She gazed into the fire until it died down to a few glowing coals and she began to feel cold. But she had no motivation to even move. Her recent thoughts and feelings were tumbling around in her mind with everything her father had just said, while she silently prayed for her internal chaos to settle into place so she could move forward with peace and confidence. She fell asleep in the chair and was surprised to wake up to the sounds of her father in the kitchen beneath the parlor. Her neck was stiff from the way she'd slept, and she was surprised she'd slept so well when she immediately realized how cold she felt. She hurried to her room to prepare herself for the day, a little taken aback to find herself smiling just to know Joseph was here and she would see him today. A peaceful calm accompanied her anticipation. Today she would make certain that Mattie was kept busy in the bakery while *she* took Joseph his meals and anything else he needed, and with any luck she might have the opportunity to get to know him better.

Joseph awakened to the distant sounds of work taking place in the kitchen and the pleasing aroma of freshly baked goods that enveloped him in a warm security he hadn't felt in years. Or had he ever? Before he'd left home, he'd never wanted for the basic necessities of life; in fact he'd been raised surrounded by huge excess of everything. But he'd never known the kind of warmth he now felt inside. He only wished it could last. He wished it so deeply he began to pray it would last, even though he knew remaining here was likely impossible once he'd healed and God might have a different path designed for his life.

After more than an hour of huddling in bed, vacillating between thought and prayer, Joseph felt restless and wished that he could make it down the stairs and be of some use. He managed to get cleaned up and dressed, although he couldn't deny how much pain still plagued him, and he was completely worn out. He sat in a chair near the fire contemplating all that had happened to bring him here and wondering where life would take him next.

A knock at the door startled him from his deep thoughts, and he called, "Come in."

He'd expected Matthew or Mattie to enter the room, but the beating of his heart increased when he looked up to see Mariah enter, carrying a tray that she set on the table next to where he was sitting.

"Good morning," she said brightly, and he sensed something different about her.

"Good morning," he replied and felt strongly compelled to just say what he was thinking and not hold back. "I was afraid you might be avoiding me."

"Why would I avoid you?" she asked and looked at the floor.

"Mariah," he said in a voice that he hoped would express some degree of how she made him feel. She looked at him, and he added, "I want you to know how grateful I am for everything you and your family have done for me, and I'm also very glad to know I can stay here and work long enough to earn my room and board. But I also want you to know that I'm mostly very pleased with the possibility of staying long enough to get to know more about you." He gauged her expression, noting that she was surprised, but pleasantly so. But he also noted that she wobbled slightly, and he wondered if his confession had affected her enough to make her knees weak. "Why don't you sit down, Mariah?" he said. "Let's talk."

She moved to the other chair quickly, as if she *needed* to sit down. He heard her take a deep breath before she turned to look at him with something warm and hopeful in her eyes that made it easier for him to keep speaking. "Tell me about yourself, Mariah. I'd very much like to know you better."

"There's not much to tell," she said with a little laugh that seemed an attempt to cover some nervousness. "You know my family . . . my work; the situation of our home. But I know *nothing* about *you*. I would very much like to know *you* better, Joseph. The life you're living does not match up with a certain . . . gentlemanly refinement. I feel like you're hiding something. I have no reason not to trust you; instinctively, I believe you are a good man. But . . . I would really like to know why you—"

"Let me assure you, Mariah, I'm not hiding anything criminal or untoward. I feel a certain . . . shame over my past, but not because of anything I did personally." The intrigue and expectation he saw in her eyes made it easy to believe he could talk about things he had no desire to talk about. But she had a right to know, and he didn't have to make it complicated. He took a deep breath and just dove in. "I grew up in a manor house so huge and lavish that I would consider it vulgar. My father is . . . or rather *was;* he passed away a few years ago—"

"I'm so sorry," Mariah said.

"No need to be. He never behaved like my father. I don't recall ever sharing any kind of warmth or tenderness with the man. You see, he was immensely self-absorbed and arrogant. The title and fortune he inherited apparently gave him the impression that he was somehow godlike while everyone around him was inferior. He treated my mother worse than he treated his children. She died from illness when I was eleven. I believe death was likely a blessing to her. My older brother was favored above me and my sister—who is now married to someone almost as arrogant as my father. But my brother was meant to inherit everything, you see. Therefore, my father actually *noticed* him, but only because there was some need to be certain that my brother was adequately educated over the fine details of inheriting the title and all of the wealth and the appropriate arrogance that my father believed was necessary to maintain such a lofty station in this world. At the time of my father's death—when everything was passed down to my brother—it was made clear to me that the allowance set aside for me according to my father's will would only be mine if I married a certain woman who came from a family of equivalent wealth and prestige. Given how I loathed this woman as much as I loathed everything about the lifestyle and attitudes that had surrounded me my entire life, I declined the allowance and left."

"Good heavens," Mariah said, a little breathless. "That's quite a story."

"It's an utterly ridiculous tale," he went on. "I look around at all the poverty and suffering and think back to the vulgar lavishness of the home I grew up in, of the parties held there, of the money spent on ludicrous trappings and extravagance . . . and I think of how all of that money could bless so many lives. But that's my past, and I can't do anything about it. There will always be the rich and the poor of the earth, and I am now among the poor . . . just trying to make enough money to survive." He sighed from deep in his chest. "I had wrongly assumed that I could make a living fairly easy since I was willing to work and work hard. But I quickly realized how the upbringing of a gentleman offers a man no valuable skills for employment." He sighed again. "So, here I am. And if not for you, I would surely have died in that alley."

"I'm very glad I found you," she said with an expression that implied a deeper meaning to her words.

Joseph smiled at her and added, "Given my situation . . . and my background . . . I was especially touched when I saw the way you pass out bread to those who need it most."

"I wish that I could do more," she admitted.

"I know. I saw that very thing on your face the first time I noticed you . . . which is exactly why I thought even then that you were the kind of woman who might actually understand why I've chosen to live the way I do as opposed to having stayed in a world of wealth and privilege . . . because my remaining there came at too high a price."

"I *do* understand," she said.

Their eyes met, and he couldn't keep himself from acknowledging what he knew to be true. "You feel it too," he stated with confidence.

"What?" she asked, but she didn't look away this time.

"There is something between us, Mariah. I felt it the first time I saw you, and now that I'm here . . . this way . . . it feels like some kind of . . . destiny. I would never impose myself upon you, Mariah; I would never take advantage of your kind charity or your father's generosity. But I cannot go another day without telling you how I feel." He saw the glisten of moisture pool in her eyes, which strengthened his confidence as he repeated, "You feel it too."

Mariah looked down then and admitted in a quivering voice, "I've never felt this way before, so I have nothing with which to compare it, but . . ."

"But?" he encouraged and instinctively reached for her hand, relieved when she didn't withdraw.

"My father is a perceptive man," she said. "I can't hide anything from him." She laughed softly and wiped her free hand over her cheeks to dry them as her tears fell. "He told me last night that . . . well," she laughed again, "let's just say he convinced me I needed to . . . get to know you better . . . as opposed to . . . avoiding you because . . ."

She seemed hesitant to try and put her thoughts into words, but she didn't need to. He rescued her from having to say anything else by kissing her hand, which made her look at him again. He smiled and simply said, "What an excellent idea. And while you're getting to know me better, I can get to know *you* better."

"That *is* an excellent idea," she said and smiled back.

Joseph was thinking he could look at her beautiful face all day when she stood and said, "Your breakfast is getting cold, and I'm certain they need me downstairs."

"Will you come back?" he asked. "When you're not so busy?"

"I will," she said and smiled at him once more before she left the room.

༄

Mariah had to stop and sit down on the stairs to catch her breath. She'd gone to Joseph's room prepared to open some conversation with him; she'd never anticipated what had just happened. And yet it filled her with such remarkable joy that she could barely breathe. The very fact that he had spoken so plainly about his feelings—at the same time she had been prepared to at least begin to acknowledge her own—added evidence to her belief that something wonderful might come of the way she felt about him.

Noise from the kitchen reminded her that she had to get back to work, and she composed herself enough to do so. Later in the day when the work was done, she went to Joseph's room and couldn't ignore the quivering in her stomach that occurred when he was so obviously pleased to see her. They talked and talked about anything and everything, sharing conversation in a way that she'd never shared with anyone—not even her father, who was so very dear to her.

Days passed with a new habit of Mariah spending every spare waking minute in Joseph's company. As he began to feel better he started joining the family for meals, and if Mariah had felt any doubt over whether or not she should consider spending her life with this man, it was erased by the way he treated her father and brother with such respect and the way they all enjoyed each other's company as comfortably as if they'd known each other for years.

A day came when Joseph insisted that he was more than fit for work, and since Christmas was not many days off, the bakery had become especially busy. Matthew taught Joseph a few basic skills that could help immensely, and Joseph picked them up quickly. Joseph joked about how efficient he'd become at cleaning the dirty dishes in only two days, but in truth Matthew was quite amazed with how quickly Joseph had naturally taken to the skill of kneading bread dough. Since it was a job that took strong arms and some endurance, Joseph proved to be very good at it.

Mariah had always loved coming into the kitchen very early in the mornings to find it warm from the fires in the ovens and her father working there. But now she found Joseph there each morning, already hard at work, and the warmth of the kitchen warmed her heart as it never had before. She prayed he would never leave; she couldn't imagine how she'd ever gotten by without him.

CHAPTER 5
Given with Love

THE DAY BEFORE CHRISTMAS EVE was always by far the busiest day of the year for the bakery. Many people had placed orders for their Christmas feasts and parties that would be picked up the following day, but most things could not be prepared more than a day in advance or they would lose their freshness. Mariah was quite accustomed to getting very little sleep during these couple of days; in fact, she and her father took turns getting some rest here and there while the others kept the ovens full and tended to. Mattie also worked hard during this time, even without needing to be urged to do so. It was a familiar Christmas routine, with the sweet anticipation of when the bakery would close late afternoon on Christmas Eve and remain closed until Boxing Day. With the exception of the Sabbath each week, Christmas was the only time during the year when the bakery doors remained locked all day and the ovens were cold. But their Christmas holiday was especially wonderful in the way they shared longtime traditions together, always mindful of the truest meaning of the holiday.

Mariah got out of bed and dressed very early on the morning of the twenty-third, so early that it was still completely dark outside. She went downstairs to get to work and found her father already busy and Joseph there helping him. They were both laughing, and she laughed a little as she entered the room; she had no idea what might have been so amusing, but their laughter was infectious.

"Good morning, my dear," Matthew said, smiling at her. Before she could answer him, Joseph smiled at her too, and she found it difficult to speak. The prospect of all the hard work that had to be done today and tomorrow suddenly felt lighter; she knew that Matthew had insisted Joseph join them for their Christmas celebrations, and she couldn't think of anything more delightful.

"Good morning," Joseph said when she just stood there and said nothing.

"Good morning," she replied and hurried to get busy with some cooled buns that were waiting to be iced.

That day and the next went by in a blur, as there was always more work to be done and they all grew progressively more tired. But Mariah couldn't help noticing that Joseph was taking his contribution to the work very seriously, and he'd become rather good in a very short time at kneading different types of dough to the right consistency and forming them into the proper shapes and sizes. Her father was a very good teacher, but Mariah couldn't recall anyone learning as quickly as Joseph. And he was obviously enjoying himself.

They all shared light conversation while they worked, and she found herself becoming more and more comfortable in his presence. It was somewhere in the midst of their work on the morning of Christmas Eve that it occurred to her how fiercely she never wanted him to leave. Now that he had been here in their home and in their kitchen, blending in so well and proving his character through his genuine humility and kindness and willingness to work, she couldn't imagine how it might be if he left. If they weren't so busy she would have told him so, but she had to put the thought on hold in order to finish up their orders.

They all remained very busy right up to the moment the last order was picked up and they finally locked the doors and closed the curtains of the bakery windows. But they had yet to bake the bread that would be distributed on the streets Christmas morning, and they had to finish baking the sugared biscuits that would be passed out as an extra Christmas treat. Once the baking was done, the biscuits were wrapped in white tissue paper and tied with a small piece of red ribbon, on which a small handwritten note was also tied. Mariah had carefully thought through what should be written on the notes, because she wanted people to realize the special meaning behind this little offering. Perhaps most people would overlook the message and not really care, but she believed some would feel its warmth in their hearts in spite of the harsh difficulties of their lives.

Mariah looked at the words she was writing and considered once again how right they felt. She had taken a well-known verse of scripture and had changed the wording slightly to make it more personal, because in her heart she knew that it *was* personal. And it was the most important message of Christmas: *For God so loves YOU that He gave His only begotten Son. Merry Christmas, and God bless!*

Mariah had already written the message on a few dozen pieces of paper she had already cut into small squares, but she had many more to write. She was pleased when Joseph sat across from her at the small table in the bakery front where she was working on her project. He smiled at her and said, "I believe I've done all I can do in the kitchen. May I help?"

"Please!" she said with exaggerated drama while she shook her right hand to try and alleviate its cramping.

Joseph read one of the notes and said, "That's very nice, Mariah; in fact, it's perfect."

"Do you think so?" she asked.

"Absolutely!" he insisted and began copying the message down with excellent penmanship.

Mariah chose to just watch him for a few minutes and give her hand a rest. Her heart began to pound as if it were urging her to speak the words that had been circling her mind since yesterday—perhaps longer. Realizing they were alone, she took a deep breath and just spoke. "It's been so wonderful having you here, Joseph. I can't imagine what it was like before, and I can't imagine how we would ever be the same if you left." He stopped writing and looked up at her. She hurried to add, "I hope that's not too bold. I thought it prudent to tell you how I feel."

Joseph set down the pen and leaned toward her over the table. "It's not at all too bold, Mariah. If I may be bold in return . . . I must confess that . . . I don't ever want to leave here. I've never felt so at home as I have here—never. Not in all my years of growing up in my family's house did I ever feel like I was . . . home." He sighed, and his gaze became more penetrating. "I don't want to leave, Mariah—not just the bakery and your family; I never want to leave *you*. A minute does not pass without my thoughts going to you; I've never known a woman like you, and I don't want to leave. But I don't want to impose, and I certainly don't want to be presumptuous or—"

Mariah put her hand over his on the table and said, "I don't want you to leave—ever. It seems we are presuming the same thing."

Joseph glanced at their hands only a moment before he came to his feet and leaned over the table to kiss her. Mariah was taken off guard but was immediately overcome with relief and perfect contentment. He looked into her eyes as if to gauge her reaction, and he apparently gauged it well when he kissed her again.

"I love you, Mariah," he whispered with his lips close to hers. "I don't know how it's possible in so short a time . . . but I do."

"I love you too, Joseph. And if you must know,"—she smiled to see the way his eyes were sparkling—"my father declares that he knew there was something special about my mother the first time he saw her, and it was only days before he knew she was the one for him. They were married within a month."

Joseph's smile broadened, but he kept his face very close to hers. "Are you asking me to marry you?"

Mariah laughed softly. "That's not my place, is it?"

"Oh, I don't mind," he said and kissed her again. "On the chance that you are, my answer is yes."

Mariah's perfect happiness threatened to burst out of her, and she feared she would either start crying with joy or laughing hysterically. Instead she quickly kissed him again then forced herself to look away saying, "We will have to talk about this later. We have important work to do."

"As you wish," Joseph said and sat back down to continue copying the Christmas message on the little pieces of paper. But he glanced up at her often as they worked, with a smile on his face that reflected her own happiness.

"What if the people we give these to can't read?" he asked after many minutes of silence.

"Oh, my goodness!" Mariah exclaimed. "How wretched of me to not have thought of such a thing; it's likely many of them are *not* able to read."

"Then we'll read it for them," he declared as if it were nothing. "We won't be in any hurry, will we?"

"No," Mariah said, already warm inside with the thought of making a tiny difference in the lives of so many who were suffering. "We won't be in any hurry. It will be Christmas day, and what better thing could we be doing?" She sighed. "I just wish we could do more."

"We will do what we can," he said as if they were completely of one mind on the matter. "And perhaps over time we will be able to do more."

"That's a lovely thought," she said, and they worked together to get everything ready for their Christmas morning excursion into the streets.

When all the work was done, Joseph joined the family for their usual Christmas Eve traditions. They shared a fine meal, working together to prepare it and then to clean up. Together they decorated the little evergreen tree that Matthew had purchased from a street vendor. With the candles lit on the tree, they played a few silly games before shifting into a more reverent attitude while they read the story of Jesus's birth from the Bible. Mariah had always loved Christmas; it was by far her favorite time of year. But having Joseph there with her and seeing how much he had grown to care for her father and brother—and the other way around—led her to believe that this was the beginning of many warm and tender Christmases yet to come.

On Christmas morning, they all bundled up and set out early, everyone carrying a basket over each arm, to pass out their offerings of bread and the little simple Christmas gifts that Mariah prayed would give the recipients even a moment of joy on this cold winter morning. They split up, with Joseph accompanying Mariah, and her father and brother heading a different direction. And they had all agreed on exactly how to go about giving their gifts with the kind of love Jesus himself might have offered if He were with them. Joy overflowed from Mariah's own heart as she watched the eyes of people brighten just a little in taking the bread and brighten more as their hands reached out to take the little treat wrapped in white tissue paper and red ribbon. With each person she asked, "Would you like me to read it for you?" And most of them did. She saw tears in many eyes as she read the simple but profound message aloud.

"For God so loves YOU that He gave His only begotten Son. Merry Christmas, and God bless!"

Sometimes Mariah expounded a little on what she believed was important to understand about the message, and sometimes she just exchanged a smile with the recipient and moved on. While she and Joseph walked through the streets together, mutually engaged in doing their tiny part to make a positive difference to the poor and suffering on this most special of all the days of the year, she felt as if her entire life was laid out before her. She could imagine doing this for years to come, with Joseph at her side and their children in tow. Silently, she thanked God for the miracle of having Joseph come into their lives and the privilege of being able to do her part to help feed the hungry. Hers was a simple life, but her heart was deeply anchored in all that Christmas represented, and she knew she had everything she needed to be happy. She considered herself to be truly blessed.

One Year Later

Christmas morning dawned with clear skies and a fresh dusting of snow on the ground. Mariah finished loading the baskets with freshly baked bread and rechecked those she had loaded the previous afternoon with what she now considered her traditional Christmas gift to pass out on the streets to anyone who might be in need of even the tiniest inkling of hope. When Mattie was all bundled up to go out, she put a basket over each of his arms and kissed his cheek, noting the smile on his face. He had quickly taken to enjoying the opportunity to go out and give bread to those in need, and given how grown-up he was becoming—and the change of circumstances for Mariah—Mattie was quite proud of mostly taking over the responsibility.

Mariah also kissed her father's cheek before she gave him two baskets and watched him walk out the door. Before she could pick up the baskets that Joseph was waiting to take, he took her face into his hands and kissed her in a way that reminded her of how very much they loved each other, and she felt deeply blessed for all the good he had brought into her life. She couldn't remember what life had been like before they'd been married; it seemed as if he'd always been a part of their family. Joseph had taken to baking as if he'd been born to it, and he'd contributed ideas to their family business that had increased the number of customers. With the bakery thriving, they were working on plans to add some rooms onto the house, which would allow enough space for their family to grow.

"It doesn't seem right for you to not be going out with us," Joseph said, "especially on Christmas." He pressed a loving hand over her well-rounded belly and kissed her again. "But it's for the best."

"Yes, I know," she said. "I'll just do as the doctor ordered and put my feet up, and I'll be thinking about you."

He kissed her once more, took the baskets, and went out the door to spread a bit of Christmas cheer. Mariah watched out the window as he walked away, noting the lightness in his step. She thought back to the first time she'd encountered him on the street when she'd been passing out bread and he'd been on his way to work at the livery. Oh, if she'd only known!

Feeling an ache in her lower back, Mariah sat down near the fire and put her feet up on another chair. She tried to relax, but the aching got worse, coming and going in waves. When the reason for the increasing pain dawned on her, she couldn't keep herself from laughing as she pressed both hands over where her baby was waiting to come into the world. Perhaps this would prove to be an especially memorable Christmas for many reasons.

ABOUT THE AUTHOR

Anita Stansfield has more than fifty published books and is the recipient of many awards, including two Lifetime Achievement Awards. Her books go far beyond being enjoyable, memorable stories. Anita resonates particularly well with a broad range of devoted readers because of her sensitive and insightful examination of contemporary issues that are faced by many of those readers, even when her venue is a historical romance. Readers come away from her compelling stories equipped with new ideas about how to enrich their own lives, regardless of their circumstances.

Anita was born and raised in Provo, Utah. She is the mother of five and has a growing number of grandchildren. She also writes for the general trade market under the name Elizabeth D. Michaels.

For more information and a complete list of her publications, go to anitastansfield.blogspot.com or anitastansfield.com, where you can sign up to receive email updates. You can also follow her on Facebook and Twitter.

OTHER BOOKS AND AUDIOBOOKS
BY CHALON LINTON

An Inconvenient Romance

"Christmas Grace" in *Christmas Grace*

A Tangled Inheritance

Escape to Everly Manor

Adoring Abigail

Christmas Grace

BY CHALON LINTON

To my grandfather,
Norman Burgess Moore.

CHAPTER 1

London, England 1813

GRACE HATED BLACK. IT DROWNED out her color and made her eyes look more gray than blue. But she loved her husband, so for the past 365 days she had donned the black silks and crepes of mourning to honor him. On the final day of the year, the one that marked the first anniversary of his passing, Grace asked her maid, Dorren, to air her dark-blue day dress. Dorren did so without question, and this morning, after opening the heavy curtains wide, Dorren pulled the blue dress from the wardrobe and laid it across the bed.

Grace walked over and fingered the richly colored fabric. She knew Julian would not mind; indeed, he'd be quite impressed that she'd worn the black for so long. But Grace had wanted to prove she could do it—that she was strong enough and Julian was important enough for her to endure the dreary color.

Besides, Christmas was a mere four weeks away. Grace didn't mind wearing black for the holiday last year, as it was the first without her husband. She had loved him and she truly mourned him. She mourned his sudden passing and the change that his loss brought. Beyond being her spouse, Julian was her friend. He was everything good and right in the world. He saw the best in people, especially Grace, and she would be forever grateful for the love he gave her.

"Are you ready to dress, ma'am?" Dorren asked.

Grace nodded and turned to allow her maid to help her change out of her nightdress. As the blue gown slipped over her head, Grace felt lighter. She would never forget Julian, she would never let him go, but she'd had a revelation the past week that would allow her to honor him and move forward with a purpose.

That was Julian's gift—giving her a purpose.

Grace left her maid with a lengthy list of instructions and set off to find her mother. Mrs. Lucille Banner was a woman who thrived on precision.

Everything had an order, and when something or someone drove that order askew, she became quite frazzled.

Grace knocked on her mother's door and was promptly bid to enter. Mrs. Banner sat in her private sitting room on a small sofa, a cup of tea in hand.

"Good morning, Mother," Grace said with a small curtsy.

Mrs. Banner gasped. "Blue? Grace, what are you thinking?" The teacup was returned to the tray immediately.

"Mr. Hershaw would hardly mind. You know he didn't prescribe to such things. It's been a year, Mother, and—"

"Only yesterday!" Mrs. Banner cut in.

"And you know it was a very somber day for me. I honored Mr. Hershaw yesterday and will continue to honor him appropriately on each anniversary of his passing. However," Grace raised her chin, "I would prefer to honor the life he lived rather than constantly mourn his death."

Grace could tell her mother bit back a retort. Mrs. Banner simply shook her head. "Grace," she said softly.

"That's why I've come to speak with you."

Mrs. Banner motioned to the empty cushion beside her then folded her hands in her lap.

Grace sat and said, "It's time I return to Hershaw Hollow."

"We agreed you should stay through the Christmas holiday."

"Being with you and Papa has been a balm to my soul. I thought coming home would help me feel better." Grace lifted her mother's hand from her lap and held it in her own. "But it hasn't." She squeezed her mother's fingers. "Do you know what made Mr. Hershaw happy?"

"You." Mrs. Banner spoke bluntly.

A blush spread through Grace's cheeks. "Yes, well, he also found joy helping others."

Grace's mother pulled her hand away. She stood and spun around. "Are you referring to the doctor he hired to watch as his former butler passed away or perhaps the fact that he gave half of your dowry to that dilapidated orphanage?"

Grace shot to her feet. "Dr. Brant offered Gibbon comfort in his final days. And the orphanage was ravished by fire, and repairs needed to be made before winter. Mr. Hershaw did what had to be done."

"No, he did what no one else would. And do you know why no one else would? Because they knew your gullible husband would sweep in and throw his money away without a care."

"You chastise me for the color of my dress, yet you stand here and disparage my late husband's name for the way he chose to spend his money? Which is it, Mother? Is he a martyr or an imbecile?"

Mrs. Banner sighed and returned to her seat on the couch. She settled back against the cushions and laid a hand across her forehead. "This discussion is giving me a headache."

"Very well. I simply came to tell you that I plan to return to Hershaw Hollow and carry on the Christmas fête in my husband's honor." Mrs. Banner sat up and stared as Grace continued. "I will be leaving at the week's end."

"But the weather continues to threaten." Mrs. Banner motioned to the window, where a steady rain tapped against the panes.

"Then I should not delay. I will inform Father of my departure so he can recommend a suitable route. Dorren will accompany me. I have many preparations to see to. Good day, Mother." Grace offered a stiff curtsy and swept from her mother's room.

CHAPTER 2

GRACE'S MAROON TRAVELING DRESS PUT her in a festive mood. Dorren had perfectly centered her dark hair on the top of Grace's head, and the adorned black bonnet nested comfortably over the twist. In March, the Hershaw carriage had carried Grace and a handful of servants to her parents' London home. Now the same entourage stood ready to escort her back to the country.

Mrs. Banner had made one further attempt to dissuade her daughter, but at Mr. Banner's request, she had finally dropped her opposition. Both of Grace's parents stood under a wide umbrella and waved a placid goodbye as the carriage pulled away.

Nottinghamshire was a three-day trip from London, but the recent rains and possible snow in the North could slow their progress. Grace was anxious to get home. Last week, when Grace had decided to continue the tradition Julian had begun, she wrote to the housekeeper, Mrs. Blaine, and asked her to begin the preparations. But she was already behind and knew she would have to work tirelessly for the next few weeks if the fête was to be a success. In truth, the demands of time were part of the appeal to Grace. If she kept busy, she would not think on the sorrow surrounding her. She would not remember how Julian radiated brightness, how when he died, Grace's light had died with him. He had made her strong. She could lose herself in a new goal to honor her late husband and the wonderful benefactor he was. Julian's Christmas fête would provide a purpose for Grace, and perhaps she would not feel so forgotten.

The rain continued the first day, but Mr. Buntly, the coachman, pressed through to the inn Mr. Banner had proposed. Grace secured the necessary rooms and then retired, anxious to continue in the morning.

After an early breakfast, the journey continued. During the first hour of the drive, Grace sat with a sketchbook balanced on her lap, and with a fat piece of charcoal, she clumsily jotted down ideas. Her final list of duties comprised four pages, due to the wide scribbled lines, but Grace grinned with accomplishment as she tucked the items back into her satchel when she finished.

"That should be a decent start," Grace said, wiping the charcoal dust from her fingers with her handkerchief. When Dorren didn't respond, Grace looked up and followed her gaze to the window. "Oh! When did it start to snow?"

Dorren turned to look at her. "About an hour ago."

"It's beautiful, isn't it?" Grace leaned closer to the window and felt a draft of cold air seep through the window seam. "It's as if the earth is dusted in white innocence. Cleansing itself before beginning another year."

Grace's memories of the past year were coated in black. Sorrow, loneliness, and guilt for her weaknesses cloaked any memory of laughter or sliver of joy. Julian had died because of his goodness. One of his tenants, Mr. Thatch, had lost his wife during the birth of their twin boys. Julian had hired a wet nurse and the boys had thrived for seven months, until pneumonia settled in their lungs and wrung their final breaths.

Julian had grieved with Mr. Thatch, forgiving the man's debts and paying hirelings to work his portion of land. But Mr. Thatch's despair had overcome his desire to live.

Grace remembered the frantic pounding at the door, the alarmed cries of the staff as Julian dressed and asked her to wait in his bed until he returned. She had settled into the blankets, confident her husband would sort out the situation. He always had, and she'd believed he always would. But hope and grief weren't such opposite sentiments.

Mr. Thatch had been in his cups that night and, with his pistol loaded, hoped to end his grief. When his neighbors had realized his intent, they'd tried to calm him and sent for Julian. Their confidence in their benefactor had been no match for Mr. Thatch's pistol.

Grace knew Julian had tried. She'd been told how he'd pled with Mr. Thatch to lower his weapon, offering him work, a room—any respite from his affliction—and in the end, money. Mr. Thatch had spat some curse about false monetary blessings and turned the gun on Julian.

Grace's hope had begun to turn fragile as the bed turned cold. Julian never returned home that night. He never returned home again, and Grace was left with the regret of her loss. Julian had never known how inadequate she felt without him. Grace had never told him how she admired his compassionate heart. She was alone, while Mr. Thatch had received his wish. One week later, he'd hung from the gallows for murder.

CHAPTER 3

GRACE STARED AT THE FALLING snow, wishing its purity could be her own. It layered onto the branches of the trees and the ledge of the carriage widow, yet she was trapped inside, unable to touch it or share in its spotlessness. Her life could never be as pure and good as Julian's had been—she'd accepted that fact—but she hoped continuing the Christmas tradition he'd begun would allow her some peace, some purpose, some tangible connection to his goodness.

Grace pressed her fingers to the cool glass but was thrown backward as the carriage jostled and a loud splintering crack rent through the silence. Both Grace and Dorren screamed as the carriage shifted again. The vehicle lurched, turning onto its side and tossing the women in a tangled mess against the door, which now lay pinned against the ground.

Hollering sounded from outside the equipage, and Grace and Dorren scrambled to right themselves.

"Mrs. Hershaw, Miss Dorren, are you all right?" Grace recognized the voice of her footman, Ethan, who'd accompanied them.

"Yes," Grace called then looked to Dorren to make sure she'd spoken the truth. Dorren gave her a nod and Grace helped lift her to her feet.

Grace yelped when the carriage shifted again, but then she looked up to see the footman's face, framed in the window that now faced the heavens. He cleared the snow from the pane and peered into the box where the women huddled together. He pulled away and spoke to someone else, though Grace could not hear the exchange.

When Ethan reappeared, he cupped his hands around his mouth and shouted through the window. "Mr. Buntly's broke his leg, and I can't turn the carriage over by myself. I'm going to take one of the horses and get help."

Grace nodded her head, and Ethan disappeared. Grace placed one blanket on the carriage door beneath them and shared the other with Dorren. Then she stared up at the window. The hope and light Grace had clung to dissipated as white flakes filled the windowpane.

⁓ℓ⁓

The carriage darkened and the snow continued to fall as cold seeped through the cracks of the carriage box. Surely, no one would be traveling the roads in this weather; Grace could only hope that Ethan had located help. Dorren began to cry, so Grace hummed every lullaby she could remember, trying to fill the silence with something besides despair. Why, when she had latched onto a purpose, did fate derail her plans? And what of Mr. Buntly? Was he exposed to the elements, or did he have some sort of shelter? Grace trembled with the thought that her coachman might perish only a few feet away from where she sat.

Minutes muted into hours. Grace pulled Dorren close, for both heat and comfort, and her maid fell asleep against her side. Grace's throat itched as she hummed the same melody over and over again, trying to occupy her mind with something hopeful and happy. Her thoughts often turned to Julian—his kind smile, his bright-blue eyes. He was joy personified, and she missed him desperately.

Grace ignored the cold cramps in her legs and closed her eyes, longing for the peace that dreams of Julian would bring. But no sooner had she resigned herself to a frozen death did she hear shouts. Someone called her name. Could Julian be beckoning her to heaven? Grace pressed her eyes firmly closed. She felt certain the voice rang solely in her mind, and she listened closely, hoping to hear her name whispered from her husband's lips.

"Mrs. Hershaw!"

Grace's eyes opened wide. Could it be? Were they saved?

The carriage swayed, and Grace wrapped her arms tighter around Dorren, though the maid remained ignorant of the tumult beyond her dreams.

"Mrs. Hershaw, are you there?" The question was followed by a repeated thump near Grace's head.

"Yes!" she cried out. Dorren's eyes blinked open. "Help me," Grace told her maid. She winced in pain as she shifted her legs beneath her and began to beat upon the side of the carriage. Dorren watched in confusion as Grace continued to pound.

"I hear them!" another voice called.

The carriage shook and Dorren grabbed onto Grace's arms. "What's happening?" she cried.

Grace's eyes skimmed the blackness for the answer she couldn't provide. The walls around the women rumbled, muffled sounds coming from every direction. Grace searched through the dark until finally, in the window above her head, the light of a lantern swung back and forth.

"Look," Grace cried out and pointed upward. "Ethan's come back."

"We're going to right the carriage," Ethan hollered. "Prepare yourselves."

Grace nodded at Dorren and took her hand. "We'll probably tumble again, but soon we'll be next to a warm fire."

The next minutes were filled with anticipation until a unifying countdown from three rang out. The rotation wasn't as abrupt this time, and Grace managed to shift her body as the carriage tilted upright. Within moments, the door opened and an unfamiliar face peered inside.

"Are you all right?" the man asked.

In the shadows of the night, Grace couldn't decipher the details of his features, except that his eyes were dark, yet kind. "Yes, a few scrapes perhaps, and we're dreadfully cold, but contrary to my thoughts these past few hours, it seems we shall survive."

The man laughed. "Indeed you shall." He reached his hand forward to assist Grace. As she moved toward the door, he said, "Mrs. Hershaw, my name is Gordon Burgess. I'm afraid the step has been damaged. Do you mind if I assist you?"

"Not at all," Grace said.

Mr. Burgess easily lifted her down, and Grace's feet settled into the cushion of snow. He addressed a man standing next to him, who held a bundle in his arms. "Martin, may I have the cloak for Mrs. Hershaw?"

Martin shook out a long fur-lined wool cloak. Before Grace could accept it, Mr. Burgess reached around her and secured it over her shoulders.

"Thank you," Grace said, grateful for the warmth that began to permeate the chill that had settles into her bones.

Mr. Burgess smiled. "You're very welcome." Then he turned and lifted Dorren from the carriage. Martin handed Dorren a cloak as well.

Grace addressed Mr. Burgess. "What can you tell me of Mr. Buntly? Is he . . ."

"He's well. Or he's alive, at least. I'm afraid he has a rather terrible break. You're servant Ethan was rather ingenious. He arranged some of your traveling trunks around the wheels and fashioned a makeshift tent for your coachman. We had to dig a bit to get Mr. Buntly out, but he only complained of the pain in his leg. I sent him to Fenwood with two of my men."

Grace pulled the cloak tight around her shoulders. "I was so worried."

Mr. Burgess reached back into the righted carriage and removed the hat Grace had torn off hours ago. "You may want this, Mrs. Hershaw. It's a bit of a ride to my home."

Grace tied the ribbons under her chin. Ethan rode forward, holding a lantern high and pulling a second horse beside him. "Here's your horse, Mr. Burgess. We'll have to come back for Mrs. Hershaw's items once the storm breaks." Grace nodded her understanding, and Mr. Burgess directed Dorren to Martin, who stood a few feet away.

He turned back to Grace. "May I, Mrs. Hershaw?"

Grace did not reply. She simply placed her hands on Mr. Burgess's shoulders as he lifted her to his horse's saddle. He swung up behind her and, without a word, turned his horse into the darkness.

CHAPTER 4

THE CONTINUOUS SHEET OF SNOW concealed the stature of the estate, but Grace immediately knew the house was grand. Her thoughts were confirmed as she stepped through the large arched doorway. The foyer was opulent. Rich marble tile variegated by a border of smooth black stone ran the length of the entrance and trailed back into the house. Despite the late hour, at least a hundred candles were lit and servants bustled around in organized chaos.

Grace's attention was drawn to her rescuer, who spoke with a thin, middle-aged, red-haired woman who appeared to be reporting to him. Although her eyes were tired, Grace took the opportunity to look him thoroughly over. His brown hair was wet from the snow, and she saw the same depth in his eyes she'd noticed when he'd pulled her from the carriage. He stood a head taller than her, and his face was sturdy, his cheekbones dipping down to the angle of his jaw.

"Mrs. Hershaw," Mr. Burgess said and stepped up beside her. "My house-keeper, Mrs. Mercer, has informed me that Mr. Buntly's leg has been set and he is resting in one of the guest rooms."

"Guest room?" Grace raised a hand to her mouth. "I'm sure Mr. Buntly does not require such extravagance."

"I wanted him to be comfortable in his recovery," Mr. Burgess said.

"That's very kind of you. Did the doctor travel here to tend him?" Grace asked.

A smile lifted the corner of Mr. Burgess's mouth. "No. My butler, Hartford, served in the British Army. He's performed the task before and saw to Buntly upon his arrival."

"And what of Ethan?" Grace asked.

"He and your maid have been taken upstairs. They will be provided with warm clothes and food, and I daresay they will soon be sleeping comfortably."

"Well then. I thank you, once again," Grace said. She absentmindedly rubbed her hands together.

"Let's get you settled as well. Mrs. Mercer?" Mr. Burgess called to the woman with ginger hair.

Mrs. Mercer stepped forward and curtsied. "I've prepared the daisy room for you, ma'am."

"The daisy room?" Grace repeated and looked to Mr. Burgess.

His cheeks darkened, and he gave a sheepish shrug. "My mother is a self-proclaimed botanist, and she has a passion for flowers. My father granted her free reign to decorate the guest rooms, and she christened each of them after a different variety of flower. When I inherited, she asked if I'd like her to redo the décor, but she's so pleased with the arrangement I haven't had the heart to ask her to change anything."

Grace couldn't say why the innocent compliance of son to mother touched her, but she found herself smiling. "Might I ask which room Mr. Buntly occupies?" Grace asked with feigned innocence.

Mrs. Mercer smiled wide. "The tulip room, ma'am." Grace couldn't help but laugh. "Come. You must be exhausted." Mrs. Mercer waved an arm and ushered Grace up the grand staircase. "All the bed chambers are on this floor." They turned right down the hallway, and when Mrs. Mercer led her into the room, Grace knew immediately how it had received its name.

A toasty fire roared warmth, and Grace admired the mural of daisies painted on the wall behind the bed. Green, gauzy drapes hung from the canopy bed, matching the rich green in the thick quilt. A variety of pillows, embroidered and beaded with daisies, lay against the headboard, and a plush brown-and-yellow-paisley carpet covered the floor.

Within minutes, Grace was dressed in a dry night rail and tucked under the downy blanket while Mrs. Mercer stoked the fire one more time before bidding her good night.

CHAPTER 5

GORDON RETIRED SOON AFTER MRS. Hershaw was taken to her room. Despite his exhaustion, he could not sleep. When a harrowed and soaked stranger had pounded on his door five hours earlier, he'd immediately agreed to help and gathered the able members of his staff to head out into the storm.

Ethan had said very little about his mistress. Only that they were traveling to Nottinghamshire and that in the worsening storm, the horses had stumbled, causing the carriage to slide across the snow and overturn. When asked if a gentleman attended Mrs. Hershaw, Ethan had informed Gordon that she was a widow and traveled only with her maid. Leaving the comfort of his home, Gordon knew the coachman had been injured and two women were trapped in the tipped carriage, both of whom he'd determined would be quite old and ugly. He had been delightfully shocked when his assumption proved false.

He would have offered his help regardless, but when the party had been located and Gordon opened the door to release the women from their imprisonment, he'd been stunned by Mrs. Hershaw's beauty; sections of her dark hair, fallen from her coiffure, framed the soft features of her heart-shaped face. Her lips were thick, and her large blue eyes emanated innocence and trust. Gordon had immediately wanted to please her.

He'd focused on his task and pushed all other thoughts aside as he rode with Mrs. Hershaw back to Fenwood. There had not been a chance to find out anything further, but there would be time enough. The storm had not let up, and Gordon lay on his pillow with a smile, knowing Mrs. Hershaw would be his houseguest for at least the next three days.

There would be nothing improper in his actions, of course, though his mother would consider the fact that he was a lone gentleman in the house with a woman to be scandalous enough. His mother doted on propriety, and despite her possible displeasure with the situation, she would be delighted to know that Mrs.

Hershaw had caught Gordon's eye. She'd been pressuring Gordon to settle down and find a wife since his father passed away four and a half years ago. It wasn't that Gordon didn't want to marry. He would, in time. But he had never prescribed to fulfilling the demands of others. He would act only when he felt it was the proper season to do so, and thus far, he'd been content to remain a bachelor. Gordon remained busy enough managing the estate and business holdings he'd inherited at his father's passing. He could pass off some of his duties to his steward, but he enjoyed getting to know the tenants. After learning of his father's business ventures, Gordon found them fascinating and now worked to finalize several investments of his own.

His time had also been consumed as he assumed responsibility for his younger sister, Helen. His mother acted as Helen's chaperone, but Gordon kept a keen eye on Helen's various suitors. He approved of her final choice. The Marquess of Talbot had courted her for seven months before proposing marriage. Their vows were exchanged only four months ago, and the couple had recently returned to Somerset after completing their wedding tour. Gordon's mother left last week to stay with Helen and offer assistance in helping her manage her new responsibilities. Gordon was due to join them the week before Christmas, if the roads were passable.

Mother Nature determined the pace Gordon maintained. Good weather equaled work, both indoors and out. But a severe storm slowed, and sometimes halted, everything—the post, news from London, and travel—thus limiting Gordon's ability to continue negotiations with his associates. So while the snow continued to fall, he could put his work aside to learn a little about Mrs. Hershaw and try to bring another smile to her beautiful face.

Gordon threaded his hands behind his head and lay in the dark contemplating all the witty things he might say to delight Mrs. Hershaw.

~⁓~

Grace woke up comfortably snuggled in an unfamiliar bed. When she blinked her eyes open and found herself staring at a pillow embroidered with a bouquet of bright-yellow daisies, the events of the previous night filtered through her mind. She pulled the blankets tighter under her chin, remembering the chill that had settled into her bones as she'd sat in the cold carriage. Then she remembered the warmth that spread through her as Mr. Burgess draped the heavy cloak around her shoulders and she'd looked into his contemplative eyes.

Grace thought of Dorren and Mr. Buntly and felt guilty that she considered going back to sleep. She counted down from five then flung the covers back, dreading the wall of cold that existed outside her cocoon of blankets. She looked toward the fire, both surprised and happy that it had been stoked and now crackled with warmth. Grace extended her hands near the flame for a few moments before she turned to pull back the curtains.

Her shoulders fell as she watched the intricate-patterned snowflakes glide onto her windowpane. In a matter of seconds, they melted to a drop of water before sliding downward and disappearing altogether.

Grace had accepted that her journey would be delayed, but every hour the snow continued to fall set her further back. Grace rubbed her hands in front of her and tried to recall the list she'd made in the carriage. Were there duties she could perform while she remained stranded at Fenwood?

Grace decided to first tend to Mr. Buntly and then consider what could be done about the fête. She did not want to bother Mr. Burgess's staff, but she did not see her clothes and could not wander about in a nightdress. Reluctantly, she pulled the bell and was happily surprised when Dorren entered only ten minutes later.

"Good morning, ma'am." Dorren set a laden tray on a table near the door. "Mr. Burgess asked his cook to keep this warm until you woke and were ready to eat." Dorren relayed the information with a suppressed smile.

"He has proved to be a proper host. We are lucky Ethan discovered Fenwood as opposed to a rundown tavern," Grace said. Then she walked over and moaned as she took a bite of warm scone. "Delicious." She finished it in three more bites. After licking her lips, she asked, "How did you sleep, Dorren?"

"Very well. As you said, Mr. Burgess is everything proper. He's been very generous to both Mr. Buntly and me." Dorren motioned to the light-gray skirt she wore. "Even had one of his own staff give me this to wear."

Grace looked over the well-made garment. "Very generous indeed."

"Yes, ma'am. Wait until you see the dress he has for you."

"Me?"

"Yes, Mrs. Mercer should be bringing it up shortly."

"Oh," Grace said and sat quietly eating her breakfast while she considered her situation.

Mrs. Mercer appeared a few minutes later holding a dress in a lovely shade of blue. She bid Grace good morning and asked how she slept while shaking the wrinkles from the dress and laying it across the bed.

Mrs. Mercer's question fell on deaf ears. Grace's attention was wholly fixed on the beautiful gown. It was a rich-blue muslin with a scooped neckline. The skirt opened to a layer of cream-colored fabric, and a matching cream ribbon trimmed the long blue edges of the top layer and the three-quarter length sleeves.

Grace stood and moved over to touch the soft cotton.

"It's lovely, isn't it?" Mrs. Mercer asked.

Grace looked at the woman. "I can't wear this."

Mrs. Mercer's smile fell. "Oh, I see. I can try to find something more suitable."

"No, you misunderstand." Grace ran her hand over the soft fabric. "This is too much."

"Oh." Mrs. Mercer's face lit back up and she lifted the gown from the bed, holding it close to Grace's shoulders. "Mr. Burgess picked it out himself. I allow it may not be ideal for the season, but I'll bring you a shawl as well. It's one of his sister's gowns. She's been recently married, and Mrs. Burgess insisted on purchasing an entirely new trousseau, so many of Lady Grant's old dresses are here at Fenwood."

"It's so beautiful," Grace said.

"And will complement your blue eyes. You'll need something to wear until your trunks can be retrieved." Mrs. Mercer pushed Grace toward the dressing table. "Come. Let's try it on."

Grace let the housekeeper help her dress while Dorren cleared her tray and left the room to return the dishes to the kitchen. "Mr. Burgess directed me to make sure you're comfortable." Mrs. Mercer quickly glanced toward the window, and Grace saw that the snow continued to fall. "I'm afraid it may be some time until the roads are passable."

Dorren reappeared, and the housekeeper left to find a shawl and slippers for Grace to use. Dorren tugged and twisted Grace's hair, rambling about the Fenwood staff and murmuring she'd heard below stairs. "Mr. Burgess's mother is the daughter of a duke. She eloped with the late Mr. Burgess and didn't care one wit that her family disowned her. Isn't that romantic?"

"Ouch," Grace cried out as Dorren yanked the hair near her ear.

Grace glanced at Dorren in the mirror and saw her wince. "Sorry, ma'am." With softer hands, Dorren tucked the strand of hair into the twist of braids on Grace's head. "Mr. Burgess's sister just married Lord Grant, Marquess of Talbot. Mrs. Burgess left last week to join them at the marquess's estate in Somerset, and Mr. Burgess is to follow in a fortnight."

Dorren finished her work. Her hands dropped, and she stood back to admire the intricate creation. Grace too looked in the mirror, turning her head sideways to catch a glimpse of her dark hair. Grace realized the deep hue of the dress really did bring out the color in her eyes, and the cream trim gave the gown a soft femininity. "Thank you, Dorren."

The maid smiled, obviously pleased with her efforts. "Of course, ma'am. Enjoy your day with Mr. Burgess." After a short pause, she added, "He's very handsome." Grace's eyes popped wide as she turned to her maid. Dorren blushed but kept talking. "I thought so last night, but when he found me this morning to ask how you were . . . well, he was more handsome than I remembered."

"Dorren! You should not say such things."

Dorren shrugged. "You know I'm not one to mince words."

Grace laughed lightly. "No, I appreciate the fact that you speak your mind." Grace looked toward the window again and sighed. "How long do you think it will be before we can travel?"

"I don't know, but there's a gentleman downstairs, likely pacing with worry over the comfort of his houseguest. It seems he'd be the best one to answer your question."

Mrs. Mercer chose that opportune moment to return with a set of lovely cream slippers and a soft matching shawl.

CHAPTER 6

GORDON SAT AT HIS DESK but could not concentrate on the papers before him. Mrs. Mercer had informed him that Mrs. Hershaw was awake, but he wondered if she had slept well. Was she comfortable? Did she need anything more that he could provide? For some reason, her comfort became of upmost importance to him.

Beyond seeing his sister settled, Gordon hadn't been so concerned over the affairs of another since his mother had fallen ill the previous winter. Thankfully, Mrs. Burgess had recovered, but Gordon had paced and fretted for ten continuous days while he waited for his mother to regain the strength to feed herself and sit up on her own.

Gordon watched the ink pool on the tip of his quill before it dripped a dark oblong stain on the receipt he'd been reviewing. With a sigh, he set his quill aside and wiped the smudge from the paper with his finger. He looked at the ink on his finger, contemplating if he wanted to soil his handkerchief to wipe it clean. A soft rap at the threshold turned his attention to the door.

Hartford offered a small bow. "Mrs. Hershaw has taken her breakfast, and I've led her to the parlor, as you requested."

"Thank you, Hartford." Without another thought, Gordon removed his handkerchief, wiped the ink from his finger, and walked directly to the parlor.

Mrs. Hershaw turned from the window at his entrance, and the first thought that came to Gordon's mind was how well the blue gown accentuated her figure. But then he looked into her eyes, rimmed red from tears that continued to fall down her cheeks. "What's the matter?" Gordon crossed the room in a handful of strides and pulled his handkerchief from his pocket before remembering he had soiled it only moments before. He looked at the stained, crumpled linen in his hand and offered an apology. "I'm afraid you've caught me unprepared for your tears."

Mrs. Hershaw touched a corner of the soiled cloth and laughed lightly as she drew her hand away and swiped beneath her eyes with her fingers. Gordon offered a smile, consoled that his pathetic handkerchief had provided a small bit of comedy.

"Forgive me," Mrs. Hershaw said, and Gordon led her to the sofa.

"I hope your tears are not due to negligence on my part," Gordon said.

Mrs. Hershaw shook her head. "No, you've been most obliging."

"Would you care to share the cause of your troubles?" Gordon asked.

Mrs. Hershaw sat quietly for a long time. Gordon watched the uncertainty flit across her features and decided it would be best to give her some privacy. He reached the threshold of the door before Mrs. Hershaw called for him to wait.

"I was just thinking about my late husband," she said softly.

"Then I'll leave you to your thoughts." Gordon bowed his head slightly, and when he looked at Mrs. Hershaw again, her blue eyes flashed with sorrow and she hung her head. Gordon wanted to assuage her despair. "Mrs. Hershaw?" He stepped forward.

She smiled, and while Gordon appreciated her effort, it broke his heart to know she hurt. He cleared his throat and spoke again. "Things were a bit hectic last night. How are you faring this morning, eh, afternoon?"

Mrs. Hershaw's eyes widened at his reference to the time, but when he grinned, she realized his comments were meant to tease. "It was a rather harrowing experience," Mrs. Hershaw said, straightening her spine.

"Indeed." Gordon enjoyed watching her emotions undulate through her expressions. "Being trapped in the carriage must have been frightening."

Mrs. Hershaw's eyelashes fluttered before she answered. "I hummed lullabies and recalled pleasant memories of my husband. If Ethan hadn't found help, or if we had perished . . . well, at least I'd be with Julian."

Gordon didn't know how to respond. He clasped his hands behind his back and simply said, "I'm sorry for your loss. You obviously loved him."

Color filled Mrs. Hershaw's cheeks. "He was a good man. And although I didn't deserve him, *he loved me.*"

"Then you are very lucky."

"Yes, I am."

Gordon waited a long minute, admiring the strength of the woman before him. He watched her settle her emotions then he spoke again. "Forgive me if I'm out of line, madam, but . . . well, is the memory of your husband the reason for your tears?" Gordon took another step forward and spoke more quickly. "I only ask because I want to make sure you're comfortable here. Is there anything more you require?"

Mrs. Hershaw's blue eyes popped up to his. "Oh, no, sir. You've been most gracious and accommodating." She rubbed one of her hands over the other. "I was upset because the weather is so disagreeable."

"The weather?" Gordon raised one eyebrow.

Her eyes grew wide, and her lips pressed into a pretty pucker. "I have to get home."

"I'm afraid it will be at least three days before the roads are cleared," Gordon said. Mrs. Hershaw's eyelashes fluttered quickly, and Gordon could see the moisture pooling despite her effort to keep her tears at bay. "Why the rush?"

Mrs. Hershaw wiped at her eyes again.

"Excuse me for a moment," Gordon said, and he bounded out of the room to locate Hartford. Once he had commandeered a fresh handkerchief and presented it to Mrs. Hershaw, he sat in a nearby chair and encouraged her to commence with her explanation.

"On Christmas Eve, Mr. Hershaw hosted a fête for the village. I've just come out of mourning, you see, and I felt that the perfect way to honor him would be to continue the tradition he started." Mrs. Hershaw dabbed at her fresh tears with the handkerchief and continued. "But if my arrival is delayed, the task will be impossible."

Gordon regarded the woman before him. She obviously felt deeply about her deceased husband, and he couldn't explain the jealousy that burned in his breast. "My mother has taken my carriage to Somerset. I planned to ride on horseback and meet her there next week. But once the storm passes, I'll secure you a carriage. My head groom is quite a fine coachman, and I will send him to accompany you in place of Mr. Buntly, who of course may remain here until he is well enough to travel."

Mrs. Hershaw merely nodded her understanding, and Gordon wanted desperately to see her smile again. "We could move him to the honeysuckle room, for maximum comfort." The comment elicited a small smile. Gordon reveled in his victory and wondered how he might stimulate another.

"Perhaps . . ." Mrs. Hershaw began.

Gordon unknowingly leaned forward. "Yes?"

A tinge of red spread through Mrs. Hershaw's cheeks. She folded the handkerchief into a small square and stilled her hands in her lap before continuing. "Perhaps I might be able to continue preparations here at Fenwood while I wait for the roads to clear? It would ease my nerves to know I am doing something of import."

Gordon couldn't help the smile that filled his face, nor the excitement that pinged through his chest. "What a marvelous idea." He moved his chair closer to Mrs. Hershaw. "Where shall we begin?"

CHAPTER 7

GRACE'S SPIRITS LIFTED AT MR. Burgess's easy manners and apparent eagerness to aid in the preparations. "You wish to help?" she asked.

"Of course. You see, I cannot ride in this storm, and it's not exactly hunting season. It would be nice to have something to occupy my time until I can return to improving my limited talents."

Grace felt a giggle bubbling up inside her at Mr. Burgess's antics. "Limited talents?" she echoed.

Mr. Burgess answered with a grin, and Grace noted how handsome he looked with a smile on his face. He smiled a lot.

"I made a list while we were traveling, but I'm afraid it's been left in the carriage." Grace turned and absently watched the falling snow as she tried to visualize the list she'd compiled the day before.

"I have an idea." Mr. Burgess rose from his chair. "Come." He walked to the door and waited for Grace to step through the threshold before he followed. "If you are going to plan, you need a proper place to do so."

Mr. Burgess led Grace to a room down the hall. Grace immediately knew it was his office because the room resembled him. A large stone fireplace sat amidst the wood-paneled walls, and a roaring fire cracked inside the hearth. Leather chairs and a couch occupied the room, and a wooden desk with a single panel of detailed carvings sat in one corner. The desk was solid, and the room emanated warmth, just like Mr. Burgess.

Grace's reluctance slipped away. Mr. Burgess insisted she sit at the desk, and he laid a piece of paper before her. He ensured the quill was properly sharpened then adjusted the inkpot to be within her reach. She pressed her lips together in thought then scribbled her first task on the paper. "We must decide on activities for the children." She dipped the quill again and wrote another line. "There should be special prizes as well."

"Are there individual competitions? Or does everyone receive a prize?" Mr. Burgess asked. "I know from experience it's difficult to be the runt of the litter. Always watching the older or bigger children claim victory." Mr. Burgess's eyebrows rose. "Although, I did make them work for it."

"You are teasing me, Mr. Burgess, for I don't believe for a moment that you were the runt of the litter."

"I've grown a bit since then." Mr. Burgess made a show of straightening his cuffs.

Grace looked him over. His confident bearing and mischievous eyes pulled the words directly from her thoughts: "Yes, you've turned out quite well." Horrified that she'd spoken aloud, Grace clamped her lips closed and looked down at her paper.

Mr. Burgess chuckled. "Why, thank you, Mrs. Hershaw. I do believe that was a compliment."

Grace ignored him and drew a line across her second item. "You're right. It's not a contest. Every child should receive something special." She rewrote the task.

Mr. Burgess propped his elbow on the arm of his chair and rested his chin in his hand. "Did you have something in mind?"

They talked of possible ideas, but Grace wanted the perfect gift. Something symbolic, to remind the children of Julian's goodness. After fifteen minutes, she declared she would sort out the children's gifts later.

Grace continued to verbalize her tasks as she wrote them down. "We must serve Christmas pudding, but surely Mrs. Blaine will cover the preparations for the food. Mr. Hershaw always lit candles and led the children in a small procession through the gardens. I'll have to ask my butler, Lowry, to retrieve the musical instruments from the attic so that we may pass them out to the little ones."

Grace tapped the pen against her bottom lip. "We must decorate with boughs of evergreen and light the yule log, of course."

"And don't forget the mistletoe," Mr. Burgess said.

Grace considered the implication of his words, and the quill faltered in her hand. "Mistletoe will be of little worth to the children," she said.

"I wasn't thinking about the children." Mr. Burgess's gaze settled on Grace.

She slowly raised her eyes to meet his. "Are you teasing me?" she asked.

Mr. Burgess merely shrugged. "Perhaps I was teasing . . . or perhaps I wanted to see you smile."

Grace's mouth fell open. "Mr. Burgess!"

He laughed and held his hands out in surrender. "I'm sorry. It's just that you have such a lovely smile. It's a shame you don't share it more."

Grace's eyes dropped to her paper and she pressed her lips together, but she could not keep her mirth completely subdued. She mindlessly scribbled on her paper, drawing angles and lines, not noticing the silence that encompassed the room.

Mr. Burgess's voice over her shoulder stilled her quill. "You're an artist as well."

Grace quickly glanced at Mr. Burgess, who now stood behind her. Her eyes shifted back to her paper and, looking down at her scribbles, Grace realized she'd drawn a star. "Julian liked stars," she said quietly. "He said they represent hope on the darkest of nights."

"Hope?" Mr. Burgess asked.

Grace turned to look at him. "Yes."

Mr. Burgess stared at her for a long time. Finally, he said, "Hope is a valuable gift."

Grace didn't respond. Instead, she admired Mr. Burgess's dark-brown eyes.

"It sounds like it will be quite the celebration," he said softly.

Grace felt her entire face light up. "It will be."

CHAPTER 8

GORDON BEQUEATHED HIS STUDY TO Mrs. Hershaw's planning and preparations and made his way to the stables. However, he didn't call for his horse to be readied. Instead, he called for the groom and stable boys.

"I've a task for you all, and it's a bit out of the ordinary," Gordon explained. "I realize the snow is still falling, so I don't want anyone wandering far. But I need you to gather sticks."

"Sticks, sir?" one of the young boys asked.

A lad a few years older nudged the younger boy in his ribs. "Hush."

"I told you it was out of the ordinary," Gordon said with a smile. "They should be no thicker than your thumb, but any length will do."

While the handful of youth looked at each other, likely silently questioning if their master had lost his senses, Gordon turned to his groom. "Martin, please gather any spare piece of leather or twine. You may disassemble any broken tack for leather strips as well."

Martin simply nodded compliance, but Ernest, the oldest of the stable hands, cleared his throat.

"Yes?" Gordon asked.

"What are we to do with these sticks?" Ernest asked.

Gordon couldn't contain his grin. "We will be making Christmas stars."

After Mrs. Hershaw retired for the evening, Mrs. Mercer presented Gordon with the pile of colorful ribbon she'd amassed. "'Tis perfect," Gordon told her.

He donned his greatcoat and accepted the basket of ribbon from his housekeeper. Oblivious to the cold, Gordon trudged through the snow to the stables to begin his project.

The boys had gathered a substantial pile of sticks, and Martin had instructed them to lay the branches across the hearth to dry.

Gordon asked for a small ax and then picked up one of the longer sticks. He extended his forefinger and thumb along the wood, then lowered it to the ground and cut an agreeable length. He repeated the process four more times before calling for the strips of leather.

He sat on a stool before a small table and laid the five sticks across one another to form a simple star. His vision took several attempts to complete, as the leather had to be wrapped with perfect tightness and precision. Martin and the boys watched him work. One of the twigs snapped and Gordon had to cut another. In the end, the points of the star were best secured only after Gordon cut a small notch into the branches where he could nestle the leather to tie it tightly. Within the hour, Gordon fastened the last bit of string to the top of a star and lifted his creation to show the observant boys.

Eager to assist, the boys formed a line for the tasks, each completing their part before passing it to the next. Those in charge of tying the star points together alternated using strips of leather and the ribbon Mrs. Mercer had provided. Eight stars were assembled before Gordon halted the work in the late hours of the evening with a promise the boys could complete more the following night.

Gordon retired with a contented grin, contemplating the ideal way to reveal his secret to Mrs. Hershaw and imagining the shape of her lips as she smiled her approval.

CHAPTER 9

DRESSED IN ANOTHER OF LADY Grant's old gowns, this one a deep green, Grace made her way downstairs. She smiled every time she spied something adorned with flowers. She'd seen numerous embroidered pillows, a mural of a fence covered in roses, and two ornate hyacinth vases. On the first floor, Grace discovered a music room with a screen painted with sunflowers. She walked over to admire the details of the orange petals.

"My sister painted that for my mother's birthday last year." Grace turned to see Mr. Burgess standing inside the doorway.

"It's lovely," she said.

"Yes, Helen is blessed in many ways. I'm afraid she took all the talent in the family, leaving very little for me." Mr. Burgess stepped farther into the room.

"I'm sure you've acquired your fair share, sir." Grace wondered at the tight feeling in her chest.

Mr. Burgess smiled. "I'm an adequate shot and I can ride reasonably well, but I'm afraid I lack any artistic or musical abilities."

Grace recalled sitting with him on his horse. She'd noticed the sure way he'd sat in the saddle and the confidence he possessed as he'd led them through the storm. Grace shivered at the vivid memory.

"Would you like me build up the fire?" Mr. Burgess moved toward the hearth.

"Thank you, but I should return to my planning." Grace meant to walk away, to leave the room, but something in Mr. Burgess's expression kept her feet rooted in place.

His head tilted slightly to one side. "Are you planning to sing carols at the fête?"

Grace's response fumbled from her mouth. "Um . . . yes, well, I hadn't actually thought about it."

"Carols are an integral part of Christmas. You mentioned instruments for the children—I'm sure they'd like to play more songs than those they sing in the gardens." Mr. Burgess motioned toward the pianoforte.

"You want me to play?" Grace asked.

Mr. Burgess's lips twitched. "Since you're here you could select a few songs for the festivities. One more thing to cross off your list."

"Right," Grace agreed and sat at the pianoforte. She didn't need to turn around to know Mr. Burgess stood behind her. She felt his masculine presence as solidly as the keys beneath her fingers. "Do you have a favorite carol, Mr. Burgess?" Grace asked.

"Gordon," he said. Grace turned and looked up at him. "Please, call me Gordon." His voice fell soothingly around her, and Grace wanted to wrap herself in the tranquility of the moment.

Her lips pursed together, and she nodded. Then she turned back to the keys and began to play "Still, Still, Still".

"How did you know?" Gordon whispered behind her.

A shiver of delight trickled down Grace's spine. She played the remainder of the song then stilled her fingers on the keys. She shifted on the bench and focused on Gordon's deep brown eyes. "It's my favorite as well," Grace said. And for the first time in a long time, Grace felt peace.

CHAPTER 10

FOUR DAYS LATER, THE SNOW had finally stopped falling, but the roads remained buried in deep drifts. Gordon could not explain his profound desire to please Mrs. Hershaw. While he wished for her to remain his guest, he also understood her motivation to return home. Thus, every day he sent Martin to scout the condition of the roads to determine when it might be safe to travel.

Mrs. Hershaw dutifully checked on Mr. Buntly and continued whatever preparations she was able to complete from afar. Gordon had helped her decide on games for the children, as well as a general outline of events.

The guests would gather at Hershaw Hollow in the midafternoon on December 24. Cold meats, cheese, fruit, and bread would be served, and the adults could visit while the children played either marbles or charades. After sunset, candles would be lit throughout the garden, where Mrs. Hershaw would take Mr. Hershaw's place and lead the children in a musical procession through the snow-strewn paths. Then all would retire to the house for a hearty meal of warm stew, wassail, and Christmas pudding before the lighting of the yule log. Mrs. Hershaw would play a selection of carols and then present the children with their gifts.

"I'm running out of time," she told Gordon. "I've nothing for the children, and the fête is only two weeks away." Moisture began to gather in her eyes. "Mr. Hershaw always cared for the children. He would have known what to do."

Feeling bold, Gordon placed a hand on Grace's arm. "Do you trust me, Mrs. Hershaw?"

"Grace," she said on a whisper.

"Grace," Gordon repeated solemnly. "Do you trust me?"

She pulled her plump bottom lip between her teeth, and Gordon wondered what it would feel like to press his mouth against those lips. He shook the thought from his head and waited for her answer.

"Yes," Grace said. "I trust you."

Gordon squeezed her arm gently. "Then leave the children's gifts to me."

Grace stood. "You shouldn't have to take this on. This is my tribute to the late Mr. Hershaw. I never meant to impose on your kindness or hospitality."

Gordon rose and on impulse pulled Grace's hands into his own. His thumbs brushed over her knuckles and his heart pounded erratically. "You insist on doing this for him, and I insist on doing this for you. Please let me."

Grace glanced down at their clasped hands. "Very well."

"Thank you." Gordon placed a kiss on the back of her fingers. He met her eyes, smiled, and then quit the room.

That night at dinner Gordon planned to present Grace with a basket of completed stars. His stable staff had engrossed themselves in the project and crafted nearly seventy decorative stars. He hoped to have one hundred finished by the time Grace left for Hershaw Hollow.

Whenever Gordon considered Grace's impending departure, a wave of melancholy swept over him. Before her sudden arrival, he'd considered his life meaningful, and he was content. He looked after his mother, managed his estate, and took time to mingle with family and friends. He'd even taken Helen to London and escorted her through the Season and afterward taken turns with his mother to act as chaperone to her and her future husband. The past year had been filled with planning a wedding, improving the estate, and researching his future investments. Gordon's life was busy, and never before had he considered his circumstance stagnant, until he'd met Grace.

After being pulled from the carriage, Grace had allowed herself only one night of rest before plunging full force into her plans for the fête. Gordon had watched her work. He admired her determination and realized that the brilliance of the situation rested in Grace's motivation. She wanted the perfect celebration in honor of Mr. Hershaw. Grace worked not for herself or for recognition. Her labors were entirely on behalf of her deceased husband and the regard she felt for him.

Gordon admired her commitment, although the realization made him jealous of Mr. Hershaw. He knew it was silly, but it could not be helped. As he watched Grace's eyes light as she described a particular detail or memory, or when she gave a specific instruction to her maid, Gordon wished he could be the subject of such devotion. Yet, he also mourned the fact that he had not prescribed himself to something with complete dedication, as Grace had.

Never had his passion been stirred to such an extent, never had he felt so deeply about a project that he'd devoted himself entirely to it. Of course, he worked tirelessly for his mother and sister and would do anything for either of them, but never had he felt such a consuming need to commit to something beyond his self-interests, until now. Grace had done that for him—opened his eyes to see the possibilities of service, devotion, charity. Yet, his budding desire to embrace such purposes was not for the cause of being charitable. He did want to please the children. Though he'd only just learned about the fête a week prior, Gordon longed for it to succeed. Yet, this type of charity was something more; it stemmed from somewhere deeper. This type of charity was veritably connected to his heart—to love.

When Grace entered the dining room dressed in the blue gown Gordon had selected the first day, Gordon's breath stilled in his lungs. When their eyes met, Grace's lips pressed upward in a faint smile. Her hands twisted in front of her as she stood for a moment, simply looking at him. Gordon wanted to stare for hours, but when Grace dropped into a curtsy, he blinked free of his stupor and moved to hold her chair.

He cleared his throat. "You look especially lovely this evening."

"Thank you," Grace answered softly.

Gordon took his seat, and any thoughts of wooden stars, snow, or celebrations fled from his mind. Thankfully, Grace seemed undeterred by his reserved behavior and fed him continuous tales of her youth.

"And as if my Latin wasn't horrid enough, Mr. Paulsen had to endure my clumsiness as well, for he also served as my dancing master." Grace laughed lightly. "I repeatedly bruised the poor man's feet until he told Father he would have to resign his position if he was to have any hope of walking without a limp."

"He truly said that?" Gordon asked.

Grace giggled, nodded her head, and covered her mouth with her hand. "Yes. Dreadful, isn't it?"

Gordon admired the woman next to him and retained only a vague remembrance of consuming his meal.

"It seemed Mr. Paulsen's patience only extended to poorly conjugated verbs and not a fumbling debutante." A flush crept through Grace's full cheeks. "Father resumed my dance lessons himself, and thankfully, Mr. Hershaw was such an exquisite dancer that he learned to compensate for my missteps." Grace offered a meek smile and lifted her goblet to her lips.

Gordon watched her jovial mood turn somber.

"Julian compensated for a lot of my mistakes," Grace said.

Gordon hated the sadness, the defeat, he saw in Grace's eyes, and he broke his silence. "Isn't that how a marriage should work? It is a partnership, is it not?

One spouse should hardly overshadow the other. Instead, husband and wife should lift each other up. Buoy one another where there is weakness and stand as a pillar to support one another's strengths."

Grace lowered her glass. "That is the ideal."

Gordon reached across the table and placed his hand over Grace's slender fingers. "And you were lucky enough to have it."

Tears glistened in Grace's eyes. "Yes," she said and flipped her hand over to grasp Gordon's. "Yes, I was."

Gordon squeezed her fingers. "Grace, would you care to dance?"

CHAPTER 11

Mrs. Mercer sat at the pianoforte, and Hartford directed the footmen to clear a small space in the music room for dancing.

Lilting giddiness spread through Grace's stomach as she watched Gordon step up beside the servants and lift the large green sofa. It was soon nestled against the wall and the carpet rolled back to reveal the polished wood floor.

Throughout dinner, Grace had laughed freely, and the release of emotion felt good. She'd told Gordon things she'd only shared with Julian. She didn't understand the connection she felt with this man, this stranger. But of course, he was no longer a stranger. He'd taken the time to listen, to hear of the pain, the love, the place she'd reserved in her heart for her late husband. Gordon had understood and accepted that. How could she ever forget Julian when he'd been such an integral part of her growth, her existence?

When Gordon proposed a dance, Grace had agreed without reservation, but now as she stood staring blankly at the empty space, her heart beat rapidly, and she wondered if it was right to feel so excited about such a paltry thing.

Mrs. Mercer played the opening bars of a country dance, and Gordon stepped forward and offered a ridiculous bow. Grace giggled and placed her hand in his. Gordon clasped his fingers over hers then spun Grace under his arm to the middle of the floor. He looked over Grace's head and nodded at Mrs. Mercer.

With his masculine confidence, Gordon led Grace through the dance and she felt herself relax. The music floated through the room, and she enjoyed Gordon's nearness as they moved and turned with the rhythm. Near the last sequence of steps, Grace lifted her right foot too early, and as she turned left, her toes clipped the back of her leg. She cried out as she careened forward, closing her eyes to shut out her collision with the floor. Within a breath, her momentum stopped.

Grace felt the solid protection of Gordon's arms encircling her body. Fearing the truth she would see, she dared not open her eyes.

"Grace," Gordon whispered. "I've got you. It's all right."

Grace bit her lip and nodded. Gordon lifted her slowly and placed her back on her feet. She felt Gordon's warmth nearby, and although Grace knew she needed to regain her balance, she continued to keep her eyes clamped closed.

Without warning, Gordon swept her into his arms, and her eyes flew open to meet his concerned gaze. She couldn't look away, even as Gordon settled her on the sofa.

She watched the rise and fall of his chest. "I didn't want you to swoon," he said.

Grace shook her head and felt her cheeks warm. "I tried to warn you about my dancing."

Grace hadn't realized they'd been alone until Mrs. Mercer stepped back into the room and handed Gordon a large basket. He offered his thanks then walked back to where Grace lay across the couch.

"May I?" he asked. Grace shifted and moved her legs forward so Gordon could sit nearby. He set the basket on the floor then reached down and plucked something from inside. Grace tried to see what he held, but Gordon's large hands masked the object. "I promised to take care of the children's gifts, do you remember?"

"Of course," Grace answered.

Gordon cleared his throat. "Well, here they are." He extended his arm, and dangling from one of his fingers hung a handmade star, crafted from sticks and bright-blue ribbon.

Grace placed her palm beneath the fragile ornament, and Gordon slid the gift onto her hand. "It's beautiful," Grace said in a whisper.

"There's an assortment of colors so the girls can choose, and for the boys we've fashioned the ties with bits of leather." He reached back into the basket and held a leather-bound star up for observation. "We've made one hundred so far . . ."

Grace cut him off. "When did you have the time? You've been helping me plan the fête and running your estate . . ."

Gordon shrugged. "I enlisted the help of the stable boys."

Energy pulsed through Grace. The stars were perfect—an ideal tribute to Julian, to the holiday, and to the miracle of hope.

"Do you think one hundred will be enough?" Gordon asked.

Grace slid her feet to the ground and leaned toward him. She placed a hand on the side of his face as tears slid from her eyes. "It will be plenty." She leaned over and kissed his cheek. "They're perfect."

With the blue-ribboned star in hand, Grace stood and walked to the door. She held the simple offering in front of her, envisioning the joy the children would feel at receiving such a heartfelt gift. "Thank you, Gordon."

"It was my pleasure," he said, and Grace smiled all the way to her room.

CHAPTER 12

THE NEXT MORNING, ONLY ONE week after Grace's arrival, Martin declared that the roads were safe. Gordon wished he could call down more snow or falsely claim that the roads were impassable, but he knew he could not. Christmas was now only two weeks away, and Grace still had a day of travel ahead of her.

Gordon sent Martin to town with the funds and instructions to secure a sturdy coach then waited for Grace to appear at breakfast so he could deliver the news. He was happy for Grace. Happy that she would be able to honor her husband and the love she had for him. Gordon wasn't jealous of Mr. Hershaw; he was only jealous that Mr. Hershaw had been blessed to be the recipient of Grace's affection. He wished he could claim the same.

Grace swept into the room, dressed in a gown of deep burgundy. Her hair was pinned atop her head, with wisps of ringlets framing her face, a face that was smiling brightly at him.

"Good morning," Grace said as Gordon stood from his seat.

"And to you." Gordon noted the healthy color in Grace's cheeks and the joy in her eyes. He could think of only one reason for her happiness. "I take it you've heard the news?"

Grace's smile faltered. "No. Is something the matter?"

Gordon forced enthusiasm into his words. Spreading his arms wide he said, "The roads are clear. You may return home. I've already sent Martin to town to make the necessary preparations."

"Oh. Well. That is something I hadn't . . ." Grace trailed off while her fingers fumbled near her middle. After a moment she stilled her hands and lifted her chin. "Well then. I'd best prepare." She gave a single nod and left the room.

Gordon clenched his jaw and watched her exit. How could an event so unexpected change his life so completely? When Grace left, so would his purpose. Her project had given him motivation to get up in the morning, to brainstorm solutions, to utilize his skills of organization and production for a worthy cause. Gordon clamped his eyes closed as the truth hit him in the ribs. The fête provided an end goal, but it was not the motivation. Grace was.

In the short amount of time they'd spent together, he'd grown fond of her. He'd come to admire her: the pout of her lips, her large doe-like eyes, her innocence and determination. He would miss her. But while Gordon wished he could beg her to stay, to spend Christmas with his family or simply with him at Fenwood, he could not. Grace had to return to Hershaw Hollow. For herself, for her late husband, for peace. And for that reason, Gordon knew he had to let her go.

CHAPTER 13

Dorren stood next to Grace, and they watched Martin tie the last of the trunks to the top of the carriage. Gordon verified the binding was secure then walked toward them.

"I believe you're ready," he said.

"Not quite." Mrs. Mercer appeared holding a basket filled with bread, cheese, and warm ginger cookies.

Grace held the basket of handmade stars, so Mrs. Mercer handed the food to Dorren. "I'll see to this and get settled in the carriage, ma'am," Dorren said.

Grace nodded, and after Martin handed Dorren into the equipage, she turned to Gordon. "How can I ever thank you?" she asked.

"Any decent gentleman would have come to your aid."

"But you did so much more," Grace whispered and lifted the basket of stars a bit higher as evidence. "There's no way I can ever repay your kindness . . ."

"Shhh." Gordon laid a finger across her lips. "Please believe me when I say the pleasure was all mine."

Grace's throat tightened and she blinked rapidly to keep her emotions in check. But the feelings roiling through her could not be contained. "Come with us," she said.

Gordon shook his head and lifted her free hand to his lips. He pressed a kiss to her fingers. "Thank you for showing me true service and charity. You've reminded me about things I had forgotten. You've been my own Christmas Grace, and for that I am in *your* debt."

Grace pinched her lips tight and struggled to keep her tears at bay. Her efforts fell short and a tear trailed down her face.

Gordon brushed his thumb along her cheek, clearing the moisture away. "Please, celebrate. Enjoy your fête, and sing a carol for me."

CHAPTER 14

THREE DAYS AFTER GRACE'S DEPARTURE, Gordon rode to Somerset to spend Christmas with his family. He enjoyed an amiable relationship with Helen and thoroughly approved of her new husband. But while the Marquess of Talbot was everything hospitable and his staff attended to Gordon's every need, contentment eluded him.

Gordon told his family about the woman he'd rescued from the overturned carriage. His mother did not scold as he'd thought she might. Instead, Mrs. Burgess watched as Gordon explained how brave Mrs. Hershaw was as she waited in the cold carriage for help to arrive. Helen clarified a few important details—Mrs. Hershaw's age and marital status—which Gordon answered. But Mrs. Burgess held her tongue and simply observed her son.

The next night, Helen told Gordon about a private ball they'd attended the week before. "Of course, Lord Grant claimed my hand for the first dance, but afterwards Mr. York asked me to dance. The poor man had two left feet."

Gordon laughed with the family and then said, "I'm afraid Mrs. Hershaw can relate."

Gordon realized he'd spoken too soon when his mother's eyebrows shot upward and she asked for clarification. Explaining the dance meant explaining Grace's personality, and once Gordon began he could not stop. Over the next hour, he told his family about Grace's late husband, her determination to throw the fête, and the stars he'd made for the children. Once he concluded, very little was said before the party retired for the evening.

⁓

Gordon always firmly insisted he'd brush his own horse after a ride. One morning after putting away his tack, he noticed one of the stable hands having difficulty calming an agitated mare. He spent the next two hours mentoring the young boy and showing him some tricks he had learned through his experience with horses. When Gordon returned to the house, the butler informed him the family was waiting for him to take tea.

Helen poured out, and the conversation became muffled chatter as Gordon stared blankly across the room. His thoughts were of Grace and how in two days' time she would be marching through the snow singing carols with the youth of her village. He wished he could have accepted her invitation, if only to observe from afar. But from the beginning, Gordon realized the fête belonged to Julian. He thought of all the ways Grace had touched his heart and hoped that in some way, he had helped her as well.

"Gordon?" He was startled back to reality and watched his mother set down her teacup and look at him in confusion. "What are you doing here?" she asked.

"What do you mean?" Gordon asked and looked to his sister for an answer, but Helen simply pinned him with a stare.

Lord Grant walked forward and clapped him on the shoulder. "I think your wise mother is telling you to leave. I believe Nottinghamshire is only a two-day ride?"

"Christmas!" Helen said and clapped her hands together.

Gordon's entire face erupted in a grin. "I'll leave as soon as I'm able."

CHAPTER 15

THE CHRISTMAS FÊTE WAS PROCLAIMED a great success. Despite the bitter night air, a comfortable warmth had filled Grace's heart as she'd led the children through the candlelit garden. It had felt as though Julian walked beside her, laughing and skipping with the merry youth.

Mrs. Blaine's food was divine, and when Grace climbed into bed well after midnight, she relished in the success of the event. She turned toward her night-stand, and her gaze settled on the handmade star Gordon had presented her. Grace acknowledged that the evening's success was due, in large part, to him. The children and their parents were enamored with the gift Grace had presented them. Each was unique, like each child, like each day. And while Grace missed Julian, she finally felt strong enough to carry on without him.

On Christmas morning, Grace walked through the empty halls of Hershaw Hollow until she reached a large framed painting of Mr. Hershaw. "I've missed you, dear Julian," she said aloud. Grace reached in her pocket and withdrew the blue-ribboned star. "Thank you for teaching me about hope."

Tears gathered in her eyes, and she swiped them away as she heard footsteps nearby. Grace's butler, Lowry, approached with a large wrapped bundle. "There's a man at the door who asked me to give you this," Lowry said.

Grace slipped the small star back into her pocket, and while Lowry held the bulky shape in his arms, she began to peel back the fabric folded around the object. Her breath caught when the final swath of muslin fell away to reveal another, much larger, star. This one was approximately three feet in diameter and was made entirely of large branches tethered together with strips of dark-blue velvet. The fabric was crushed and creased from where it had been pulled tight around the five points.

"Who did you say delivered this?" Grace asked.

"A gentleman arrived with Mr. Buntly just now. Said he preferred not to give his name until you'd opened his gift." Lowry stood laden with the star, waiting for Grace's instructions.

"He's still here? Where?" Grace dropped her hand from the velvet and moved swiftly around Lowry. She lifted her skirts to quicken her steps and walked through the archway to see Gordon standing before her.

Grace's feet stopped moving, and she stared at him, wondering how he came to be at Hershaw Hollow. Gordon took a step toward her, his deep brown eyes never straying from hers. "Hello, Grace."

Grace's heartbeat ricocheted through her chest, and she could not form a reply.

"I hope the fête was a success." Gordon took another step forward.

Grace mumbled a weak response that it was.

A disarming smile spread across Gordon's face. "I'm sorry I couldn't bring your gift to you earlier."

Lowry arrived, trying to situate the star as he moved down the hallway. He peeked around one of the points. "Ma'am, I'm sorry I was not here to make proper introductions."

"It's all right, Lowry," Grace said with a small laugh. "I'm acquainted with Mr. Burgess; he's the one who rescued me. Perhaps you might find a place to hang his gift in the dining room. Maybe above the mantel?"

"Yes, Mrs. Hershaw. I'll see what I can arrange." Lowry bowed awkwardly around the star and hefted it down the opposite corridor.

Grace turned her attention back to Gordon. "It's a lovely gift."

"You said stars remind you of hope," Gordon said.

Grace nodded. "Mr. Hershaw taught me that."

"Do you believe it?" Gordon stepped closer so there was only a foot between them. "Because I think he was a very wise man."

"Yes," Grace said, breathlessly. "He was."

Gordon reached forward and lifted Grace's hand in his. "Grace, you've given me hope. Hope for a future I didn't know I could have. Please tell me if my hope is unfounded."

"I thought I'd lost my chance at happiness." Grace pulled her fingers free and removed the small star from her pocket. "But then I was given this." She turned over Gordon's hand and placed the familiar gift in his palm. "And if this tiny star can give me hope, I imagine a prodigiously large one can provide even more." Grace's lips turned up in a smile.

Gordon lifted his free hand and trailed his fingers down Grace's cheek. "I'll make you a star as large as a carriage. All you need to do is ask."

"I think I'll just treasure this one." Grace lifted her star from Gordon's hand and placed it back in her pocket.

When Gordon took both of her hands in his, Grace looked up at the arch overhead, and Gordon followed her gaze. "Mistletoe," he said with delight. "I thought you said the children didn't need it."

"They don't." Grace smiled and felt her cheeks flood with warmth.

"May I kiss you, Grace?" Gordon whispered.

"Please do."

Gordon's hands cradled her face, and Grace's eyes fluttered closed as he leaned toward her. Then his lips met hers. Soft. Tender. Hopeful. And Grace saw stars.

AUTHOR'S NOTES

- There was a great blizzard in England in 1813, although circumstances have been altered for use in this story.
- The melody we associate with "Still, Still, Still" was an Austrian lullaby, first written in approximately 1810. The lyrics of the song have varied through the years, but the version we now sing is attributed to Georg Götsch. The song first appeared as a carol when published with a collection of music by Maria Vinzenz Süss, in 1865.

ABOUT THE AUTHOR

CHALON LINTON WAS FIRST INTRODUCED to the Regency era by a dear friend, and now she can't get enough of handsome men in tailcoats. Chalon's intrigue in the genre stems from a nostalgic longing for manners, wit, and true love. Fortunately, she found her dashing gentleman, married him, and now lives happily ever after in Southern California.

You can learn more about Chalon's books at chalonlinton.com.
Twitter: @LizzyLint26
Instagram: lintonloveslife
Facebook: Author Chalon Linton